"Who do you think you are—Miss Marple?"

"Well, Shelley, somebody has to get to the bottom of this, and I don't have much faith in our friend Detective VanDyne, do you?"

"It *is* his job, you know."

"I know that, and he's probably pretty good at it, but this has to do with private things. Do you think anybody's going to tell him—a man, a cop, an outsider—why they were being blackmailed?"

Shelley fished her keys out of her purse, started the car engine, and backed out of the driveway at a much higher speed than was usual for her. "Probably not. No more than they're going to tell you, Jane."

"Yes they will . . ."

Bantam Books offers the finest in classic and modern American murder mysteries. Ask your bookseller for the books you have missed.

Rex Stout

Broken Vase
Death of a Dude
Death Times Three
Fer-de-Lance
The Final Deduction
Gambit
The Rubber Band
Too Many Cooks
The Black Mountain

Max Allan Collins

The Dark City

A. E. Maxwell

Just Another Day in Paradise
Gatsby's Vineyard
The Frog and the Scorpion

Joseph Louis

Madelaine
The Trouble with Stephanie

M. J. Adamson

Not Till a Hot January
A February Face
Remember March

Conrad Haynes

Bishop's Gambit, Declined
Perpetual Check

Barbara Paul

First Gravedigger
But He Was Already Dead When I
    Got There

P. M. Carlson

Murder Unrenovated
Rehearsal for Murder

Ross Macdonald

The Goodbye Look
Sleeping Beauty
The Name Is Archer
The Drowning Pool
The Underground Man
The Zebra-Striped Hearse.
The Ivory Grin

Margaret Maron

The Right Jack
Baby Doll Games
One Coffee With
coming soon: Corpus Christmas

William Murray

When The Fat Man Sings

Robert Goldsborough

Murder in E Minor
Death on Deadline
The Bloodied Ivy

Sue Grafton

"A" Is for Alibi
"B" Is for Burglar
"C" Is for Corpse
"D" Is for Deadbeat

Joseph Telushkin

The Unorthodox Murder of Rabbi Wahl
The Final Analysis of Doctor Stark

Richard Hilary

Snake in the Grasses
Pieces of Cream
Pillow of the Community

Carolyn G. Hart

Design for Murder
Death on Demand
Something Wicked
Honeymoon With Murder

Lia Matera

Where Lawyers Fear to Tread
A Radical Departure
The Smart Money
Hidden Agenda

Robert Crais

The Monkey's Raincoat

Keith Peterson

The Trapdoor
There Fell a Shadow
The Rain

David Handler

The Man Who Died Laughing
coming soon: The Man Who Lived
by Night

Marilyn Wallace

Primary Target

Al Guthrie

Private Murder

GRIME
AND
PUNISHMENT

Jill Churchill

BANTAM BOOKS
TORONTO · NEW YORK · LONDON · SYDNEY · AUCKLAND

GRIME AND PUNISHMENT

A Bantam Book / February 1989

ISBN 0-553-27646-8

Published simultaneously in the United States and Canada

PRINTED IN THE UNITED STATES OF AMERICA

KR   0 9 8 7 6 5 4 3 2 1

GRIME
AND
PUNISHMENT

Chapter One

The alarm went off at 6:10 A.M.

There had been a time when Jane Jeffry "hit the deck running." But that was ten years ago, back in the days when the children were small and she still held the naïve belief that motherhood had an achievable standard of perfection.

But since then, she'd learned that children don't necessarily grow up warped just because Mom can't find it in her heart to be peppy and bright before the sun has come up. They aren't exactly treasures themselves in the early hours. The most important thing she'd learned over the years was that there was no way to be a perfect mother and a million ways to be a good one. "Hitting the decks running" wasn't a requirement.

She staggered to the bathroom and tried not to meet her own gaze in the mirror. Bathrooms should never be equipped with mirrors or lighting fixtures after their tenants passed the age of thirty, she felt. She peeled off her T-shirt-style nightgown that said "Somebody in Chicago loves me" across the front. The kids had given it to her for her birthday.

As she came out she met her daughter Kate coming in. "I'm out of toothpaste." The thirteen-year-old's grieved tone suggested that her mother had deliberately squeezed out the last bit just to inconvenience her. "Mom, aren't you ready yet? I'll be late."

"Katie, it's only 6:15 in the morning. That's *not* late by anybody's standards. There's not a single thing of importance that's ever happened this early. Ever. In the whole history of the world," Jane said, slipping into a pair of jeans.

"Oh, *Mother!*"

"Hold it! Give that toothpaste back. Are Todd and Mike up and moving?"

"I don't know. Are you really wearing *that*?"

Jane looked down at the sweat shirt she'd pulled over her head. No stains, no frays, no messages, obscene or otherwise. "Why not? Who's to care?"

"Everybody'll see you!" Katie wailed.

"Katie, 'everybody' is a bunch of other half-asleep mothers who have also stupidly allowed themselves to be dragged into the cheerleading practice car pool. We'll *all* be ashamed of ourselves. There is no eye contact in the junior high parking lot at 6:30 A.M. Take my word for it."

"Ellen Elden's mother always has on makeup and a skirt."

It was Jane's opinion that Ellen Elden's mother didn't have the sense God gave a macadamia nut. If she did, she'd have given her daughter a sensible name instead of something that sounded like a musical tongue twister.

"Put that toothpaste back where you found it. With the cap on," Jane warned as she hastily dragged the bedclothes back into order. Tomorrow, when she tried out the new cleaning lady, she'd strip the bed. Maybe the woman would be able to do a neater job of putting it together than she could. Somehow the bed had never gotten into this kind of mess when she was sharing it with her husband Steve, not even when they made love. Of course, if they'd made love in such a way as to wreck the bed, he might still be in it.

Seven months now, and she still couldn't get through a day without thinking about him.

She was ready to go downstairs, but paused for a minute before starting down and listened suspiciously to the quiet. She could hear Mike's alarm buzzing faintly and banged on his door. "Rise and shine, kiddo! You've got marching band practice before school," she shouted, waited for the answering groan, then went to the next room. This door wasn't closed. It was Todd's room, and he hadn't reached the age where he wanted to shut his mother out. In fact, given half a chance, he'd have just camped out at the foot of Jane's bed and abandoned his own room altogether. During thunderstorms this was, in fact, her ten-year-old son's modus operandi.

She gazed fondly at him for a minute. "Todd, honey, time to get up," she said, ruffling his blond hair. Willard, their big yellow dog, was sleeping between Todd and the wall. Belly up, paws the size of coffee mugs stuck straight into the air, he thumped his tail and made a pleasant dog groan in greeting.

"MOTHER!" Katie shouted from downstairs.

"Yes, yes."

As she flew through the kitchen, Jane noticed that Katie had spilled some milk on the counter (which one of the cats was obligingly licking up), left the donut box open, and hadn't put the carton of orange juice back in the refrigerator. Oh, well, the boys would just mess it up again by the time she got back, she thought as she rummaged in her purse for the car keys.

Katie was in the station wagon, waiting impatiently. The garage door was still closed. Jane got in the car, adjusted the rearview mirror and latched her seat belt, then sat back. "*Someone* needs to open that door. You didn't think about that, I guess, as you walked by it."

"Oh, *Mother*," Katie said, getting back out with a world-weary sigh. This was something they had gone through nearly every morning last school year. Somehow Jane had hoped this year would be different.

On the way to school, Katie reopened a too-familiar subject. "It's our allowance day, remember?"

"Uh-huh," Jane said, stopping behind a trash truck that was stopped in the center of the road to facilitate loading from both sides. Jane smiled. Once last year her friend Shelley had gotten stuck behind one of these smelly, inconsiderate monsters that was halted in front of her own house blocking traffic. Already running late, Shelley had laid on the horn, and when the driver leaned out and made a rude gesture, Shelley had promptly pulled around the truck, right through her yard, and left the trash men gaping with surprise. Jane had often wanted to do the same, but driving through somebody else's yard might not make her very popular with the neighbors.

"You're giving me an extra ten dollars, remember?"

"I am? What for?" Jane asked, tapping her fingers on the wheel and craning her neck to see what they were doing that took so long. One of the trashmen was riffling casually through a stack of *Playboys* that someone had tried to throw away.

"The tanning sessions."

Jane honked the horn. "No way."

"But you *promised*!"

"I didn't promise. I said I'd think about it. I have. It's too much money, and dangerous besides."

"Dangerous!" Katie scoffed.

"You'd have skin cancer by the time you're thirty-five."

Katie flounced magnificently. "Thirty-five! Who cares by then?"

"You will. And you'll blame me."

"Oh, Mother! I'll be the color of a polar bear by November if I don't go."

"No-go, kid. Sorry."

The trash truck finally pulled over, and Jane realized it was because they'd blocked a businessman who'd come from the opposite direction. *He* was worth moving for. "Male chauvinist pigs!" Jane muttered.

She joined the line of station wagons disgorging girls in front of the junior high. Jane discovered that her predictions about there being no social contact this early were wrong. School had only been in session for three rainy autumn days, and this was the first sunny morning. Today, several of the women were out of their cars, chatting with each other. Two were dressed in sporty tennis dresses and carrying rackets. Katie glanced at them and then raked her mother with an I-told-you-so glare.

"Out!" Jane ordered.

"Think about the tanning sessions, Mom."

"I have. No. Close the door."

The boys were dressed and watching cartoons at the kitchen table when she got back at 6:50. Mike, a gangling fifteen-year-old, swallowed the last of his orange juice and shoved back his chair when she came in the door. Through the donut he'd stuck in his mouth to free his hands, he said, "Where you been?"

"Stuck behind the garbage truck. Ready?"

Mike mumbled something that might have been, "Just about."

Jane sat down for a second in the crumb-spattered place he'd left and prodded her youngest gently in the ribs. "Hey, Todd, old thing, haven't you got anything to say for yourself?"

He tore himself away from a vision of a badly animated character flying between buildings. "Hey, Mom, old thing. I need three dollars to get some colored pencils at school. The teacher said we had to have them for maps today."

"Three dollars? Why didn't you tell me yesterday? I could have picked them up at the store."

He grinned. "I guess I forgot."

If Katie, or even Mike had given her that line, she probably would have been irritated, but with Todd—well, it was different. He was still her baby. At ten, he hadn't started to develop the apparent contempt Katie had for her. Jane had no doubt he'd get to that stage in good time. Even Mike, the most sensible and even-tempered of children, occasionally showed signs of it.

She remembered vividly how she'd felt about her parents during her early teens. She'd been sure they were the frumpiest, most embarrassing individuals in the world. She was nearly twenty before she began to realize that they were actually quite interesting, sophisticated people. Most of the time she felt certain her children would come back to liking her when they grew up. But Todd still thought she was okay, and she wanted to hang onto that as long as possible. She needed unreserved love right now more than ever.

Mike shuffled back through the kitchen balancing a backpack of books and a battered tuba case. Somehow he freed a hand long enough to stuff another donut in his mouth. "Mmrphh?" he asked, looking at her and then at the door.

"Sure," Jane said, opening it and getting out of the

way while he maneuvered through. Willard tried to make
an escape, which Jane thwarted with her knee. He backed
off with a "well, it was a good try" look and collapsed
pitifully in front of his empty food bowl.

Thinking she might fool Mike, Jane started toward
the driver's side of the car, but Mike spit the donut out in
the driveway and said, "I'm driving."

"Mike, don't throw that food there!"

"The birds'll eat it."

Jane got in on the passenger side, wishing she had a
crash helmet. "Have you got your learner's permit with
you?"

Mike just rolled his eyes in exasperation and threw
the car into reverse. They shot backward, Mike grinning,
Jane with her hands splayed on the dashboard. Someday,
she told herself, she'd remember this time fondly, but not
anytime soon. Mike's driving made her crazy. This was the
sort of thing Steve ought to be here for; teaching a boy to
drive was "Dad work." It wasn't that Mike drove all that
fast—well, only in reverse—but he was a curb-clipper.
After sixteen years of perceiving the road from the passenger seat, he liked the same view, even though he was now
sitting four feet farther left. "Watch the jogger!" Jane
shrieked.

"I see him," Mike assured her placidly, swinging out a
generous four or five inches to the left.

They stopped and picked up Ernest, a tubby, pimpled
boy who tossed a trombone case in the back of the wagon,
and Scott, a tall, California-blond, and altogether shockingly
handsome boy who carried no books, only a pair of drum-
sticks. He bounced into the seat behind Jane and beat an
affectionate tattoo on her shoulder. "Hi, Mrs. J. Lovely as
always," he said, lifting a portion of her uncombed hair
with a drumstick.

Jane half-turned. "I'm more concerned with internal
beauty, Scott. Of which I have loads, I might add. Mike!
That truck is stopped!"

The high school was in the opposite direction from
the junior high, and the time lapse had given the same
trash crew time to get in her way twice in one morning.

They'd probably get some kind of award for that, she thought.

"Plenty of room," Mike said, going around it with a fraction of an inch to spare.

"Excellent!" Scott said and beat out a happy rhythm on the window.

Someday I'll have hysterics or wet my pants or something equally embarrassing while riding with him, Jane thought. He'd have a regular license someday instead of a learner's permit, and she wouldn't have to ride with him anymore. He'd still do awful things with the car, but she wouldn't have to ride along and be a terrified witness.

Once the boys were out of the car, Jane was stranded in a snarl caused by a mob of girls surrounding a red Fiat. The high school parking lot made her strangely sad. These boys and girls on the verge of adulthood were all so young and healthy and beautiful. Even the plain ones had a wonderful vitality. But it wasn't their youth that saddened her. She was handling the march of time fairly well. It was their air of "belonging" that she envied. They waved and called to each other and moved in graceful shoals, like happy fish. The boys punched each other's arms in a friendly way; the girls put their heads together, sharing secrets.

Jane had missed all that. A State Department brat, she'd never attended the same school more than a single year, and several times had been only a semester in one place before her father's assignments moved them on. There had been benefits, of course. She'd lived all over Europe and much of the Far East, not to mention both east and west coasts of the United States. But those were the kinds of advantages that only the adults who chose such a life could appreciate. To a naturally shy child, it had been agony.

At least she'd spared her children that unhappiness, she thought as she squeezed through a group of boys noisily tossing a basketball back and forth over passing cars in the parking lot. Her kids had all been born here and had lived in the same house all their lives. When they left their familiar neighborhood, it would be because they wanted to, not because they had to.

There wasn't a lot she was willing to give Steve credit for, but thank God he'd left her with barely enough money to keep them in this secure life and neighborhood with a full-time mother. They'd never be able to keep up with the Christmas-in-the-Caribbean crowd, but at least they weren't going to have to move into a crackerbox rental house and sell off the china to make ends meet.

Todd was sitting on the front steps when she pulled into the drive. Just behind her a blue Mazda stopped and honked. The driver hopped out. Dorothy Wallenberg had on a tennis skirt and neon-pink blouse. She was a plump, solid woman who had thighs like tree trunks—well-tanned, well-muscled tree trunks. Dorothy always seemed to be in a hurry, and this morning was no exception. "Hi, Jane, do me a quickie favor, will you?" she said, bounding around to the trunk of her car and gingerly lifting out an enormous sheet cake. "Take this in to Shelley, please."

Jane slapped her forehead. "For the meeting tonight! I'd forgotten. I promised her I'd make a carrot salad. She'll skin me for not having it ready."

Jane's friend and neighbor Shelley had a wonderful house for entertaining and did a lot of it. Almost any group she belonged to could count on her house for meetings and parties, but she despised potluck dinners, and when she was forced to have one she managed it like a parole officer. Nobody got to just wander in at their leisure, bringing their food. The food came first, early in the day; the guests could then arrive as late as they wanted without interfering with serving the meal. That was Shelley's standing rule, and it was a measure of the strength of her personality that her friends had learned to honor it.

"Thanks!" Dorothy said, easing the pan onto Jane's waiting arms.

"You're coming tonight, then?" Jane asked. Dorothy had previously claimed a schedule conflict. A former nurse, she volunteered in a free birth control clinic several nights a week.

"Sure," Dorothy answered with a grin. "Life isn't all vaginas."

"Mostly, though," Jane answered.

Dorothy laughed and got back into the car. "All settled, kids? Jane, there's a donut on your driveway."

"I know. Flocks of ravenous birds are due any minute."

Her hands occupied with the big cake pan, Jane stuck
out her leg and waved good-bye to Todd with her foot. He
rolled his eyes and looked away.

A bad sign, that. A symptom that the beginning of the
end was in sight.

Chapter Two

Keeping a firm grip on the sheet cake, Jane went to the side entrance of Shelley's house next door and leaned her elbow on the doorbell. Just then a van pulled up in front. Across the side of it in blue letters was the message: *Happy Helper Cleaning Service*. A thin woman in her thirties with frizzy blond hair got out and waved good-bye to the driver and other passengers. She was wearing something polyester that looked like a nurse's pantsuit dyed light blue. Across the breast pocket it said *Happy Helper*.

"You must be Edith," Jane said as the woman joined her on the porch.

"No, I'm Ramona. Are you Mrs. Nowack?"

"No, but this is her house. I'm Mrs. Jeffry from next door. Ring the bell again, would you?"

Shelley, immaculately turned out as always, opened the door a moment later. Her sleek, dark hair looked like she'd just stepped out of a very expensive beauty shop, and her navy-blue sweats—which Jane had seen her purchase at K Mart—looked like something a designer had whipped up especially for her. Shelley had a way of doing that to clothes.

"Mrs. Nowack?" the Happy Helper asked.

"Yes? I was expecting Edith. Hi, Jane."

"I know, ma'am, but Edith took sick and they sent me instead. They tried to call you from about six this morning, and the line was busy. If it's not okay, I can call and the van'll come back for me."

Shelley obviously wasn't pleased, but said, "No, I

need the help today and I'm sure you'll do a fine job. Come in. I wonder what's the matter with the phone. The dog must have pulled the basement extension off the table again."

Both Shelley and the Happy Helper stood aside and allowed Jane room to safely negotiate the door with the unwieldy cake. "I didn't get your name," Shelley said to the cleaning lady.

"Ramona Thurgood, ma'am."

"I'll show you where everything is, Ramona, so you can get started."

Jane leaned against the counter, studying the kitchen and wondering how it could possibly look cleaner. Shelley had the sort of house that Jane's mother would have said you could eat off the floors in—if you didn't mind the taint of fresh wax and Lysol. As many years as she'd known Shelley, Jane had never figured out just when Shelley did all that cleaning. She'd never caught her at it. Once she'd appeared at the door with a dustrag in her hand, and occasionally Jane was able to discern the scent of fresh furniture polish, but she never actually *saw* Shelley clean anything.

But then, there was a lot she didn't understand about Shelley. They'd become friends, Jane supposed, more through geographical proximity than natural inclination. Over the years, they'd come to spend a lot of time together and had a frank, friendly relationship, in spite of the fact that they were very different. But if they hadn't lived so close, Jane wasn't certain she'd have ever learned to like Shelley so well. She was a little too perfect, a smidge too attractive, a bit too bossy and self-assured for most people to warm up to her.

"You weren't supposed to make a cake," Shelley said when she returned to the kitchen a moment later. "I assigned you a carrot salad."

"I know you did, and it's in my refrigerator," Jane said.

"Yes?" Shelley cocked a shapely eyebrow.

"Well, it will be as soon as I fix it. This is Dorothy Wallenberg's cake. How is it that you can wear a paisley scarf with a sweat suit and look like a model? I wrap a scarf around my neck and I look like Dale Evans."

"Don't be a dolt. You could wear anything if you could just believe in yourself. You looked great last week in that green dress with the gold scarf."

"Only because *you* came over and tied it for me."

"Put that cake on the counter. You're getting icing on your shirt. Frenchy! Stop that!" she added as a tiny orange poodle came tearing around the corner, legs whirling like a cartoon dog on the slick floor. He sank his teeth into Jane's pant leg.

"He really thinks he's a fierce beast, doesn't he?" Jane said, shaking him loose. "Big old Willard would be afraid to attack a piece of notebook paper, and this little thing thinks he can bring me to my knees."

"He's going to the kennel this morning. I'm not having him ripping everyone's hose tonight and shedding all over—"

"Poodles don't shed," Jane said.

"Whoever told you that was trying to sell you a poodle. That reminds me, I didn't show that woman where the vacuum cleaner is. Won't be a sec. Pour us some coffee, would you?"

Jane had their coffee ready and had also put out a plate of cookies when Shelley got back from the basement. Jane was having her first cigarette of the day. She'd been cutting down slowly for months, half-intending to take a plunge into quitting, but not ready yet. This month she was allowed twelve a day: four each in the morning, afternoon and evening.

"I assume you got the kids off yesterday. How do you think they'll like Disney World?" Jane asked when Shelley sat down.

"They'll like it fine. It's the principal who's hating it. He tried to tell me the only excused absences were for family trips, and I told him they *were* with family, my sister's family. Silly man started carrying on about the sanctity of the school day—"

"He didn't!"

"Well, not in those terms, exactly, but it was pretty

haughty stuff, so I made him look up their grades and he settled down a little."

Brilliant students, Shelley's kids brought home report cards that made Jane's mouth water.

"So when do they come back?"

"Not till Sunday night, but I've got to go to the airport today. To think, when we bought this house I knew how far it was from O'Hare, and I didn't think that would matter! What a fool."

"If the children aren't coming home, why are you going clear out there?"

"My mother's going to Hawaii, and she beat some poor, downtrodden travel agent into scheduling flights so she'd have two hours stopover for lunch with me and another two hours for dinner with my brother Fred in Los Angeles. Here, eat this instead of the cookies," she ordered, taking a bowl of tapioca out of the refrigerator.

"Yuck!"

"I've got to get the middle shelf cleared so everybody can put their food for the potluck in while I'm gone. I'm really irritated about the Happy Helper people sending this woman. I hate leaving someone I don't know a thing about in the house when I can't be here."

"You don't know Edith either. You've only had her clean for you once before, haven't you?"

"Yes, but I know *of* her from the other people around here she's been with for ages. Actually, I'd be glad to try someone else if I didn't have to leave the house. I wasn't all that impressed with the wonderful Edith. I know everybody raves about her, but I didn't think she was so great. She smudged up more windows and mirrors than she cleaned, and I know for a fact she didn't even touch the kids' bathroom."

"How odd. Robbie Jones and Joyce Greenway swear by her, and Joyce is probably the most compulsive tidy person I've ever known—next to you, of course," Jane added.

Shelley regarded her mania for cleanliness as an affliction. "I know it's shallow of me, but I really love to clean," she'd said once. "You know my favorite shopping place in the world? The hardware store—the section with the industrial cleaners and mops and buckets. I sneak in sometimes just to look at the new products." Shelley was the only person Jane knew who actually apologized for her house being so immaculate.

"I hope Edith isn't sick or something," Jane went on. "I'm supposed to have her at my house tomorrow for the first time. I've never even seen this wonder woman."

The previous month Jane and Shelley's regular cleaning lady had decided to give it up and go live with her married daughter in Little Rock, after being with them for years. Shelley had immediately set about finding a replacement. Edith had recently lost two of her regular customers, and Shelley got her for Thursdays and arranged for Jane to have her Fridays.

Jane had originally decided not to get anyone, thinking she could do it herself and save money. Then she found out what sort of housekeeper she really was. Within two weeks it looked like a band of cossacks had been using the house.

"I could come over and keep an eye on your Ramona, I guess. If you're worried about leaving a stranger in the house," Jane said.

"And what reason would you give for hanging around here all day when you live just next door?"

"There is that."

"Don't worry, Jane. It'll be fine. If she goes off with the silver, I'll worry about it later. The Happy Helper people are supposed to be bonded. Wouldn't you eat some of that tapioca?"

"Not if you set my hair on fire."

Jane cleaned up the kitchen when she got home, a slap-dash clean because the great Edith—or a substitute—would be along soon to take care of the residue. Max and Meow all but clung to her legs, howling pitifully for cat food while she worked. Willard simply sprawled, snoring, underfoot. She got them all fed, then started looking around for the ingredients for the carrot salad. Shelley had given her the recipe, but she'd lost it twice already and was afraid to admit to such chronic domestic carelessness. Not that Shelley would be surprised, of course.

Jane was fairly certain she remembered it, though. Sliced carrots ("Fresh and cooked just to tenderness, Jane. Not those orange plastic circles they sell in cans."), some onions ("Sliced paper-thin, not hacked-up chunks like you do in meat loaf. Your meat loaf always looks like Attila the Hun had a part in fixing it."), and some sort of sauce. That was going to be the tricky part, faking a sauce. To the best of Jane's recollection, it was based on some sort of salad dressing—Italian, most likely—and had some strange liquid added. Orange juice, Jane thought. Or maybe lime.

Well, she didn't have any carrots, so she'd have to hit the grocery store before she could begin. Who gave Shelley that recipe anyway? Jane closed her eyes, trying to remember where she'd had the dish. She could visualize the yellow bowl with the scalloped edges that the salad had been in . . . the tablecloth with the leaf motif . . . ah! She'd had it at Mary Ellen's! Surely she'd know the recipe.

She dialed, and on the third ring, a soft, husky voice answered.

"Mary Ellen? Jane Jeffry. Hope I didn't disturb you. I wondered if you had that carrot salad recipe. Shelley gave me orders to make it for tonight, but I've lost the recipe."

"I've got *a* recipe, but it might not be the same. Why don't you just get it from Shelley?"

"She's gone for the day, or getting ready to go if she hasn't left yet," Jane said, unwilling to admit she didn't want to face Shelley's wrath.

"Oh, yes. To have lunch with her sister or something at the airport. She told me Monday, when I was collecting for the Cancer Society. Just a minute—my buzzer's going off."

"I'll just run over and get the recipe."

Jane peered out the kitchen window. Good. Shelley's minivan was gone. But, just in case, she sprinted across the street to Mary Ellen's house and lurked behind the tall evergreen next to the door until Mary Ellen let her in.

Mary Ellen was a real beauty. Her appearance was stereotypically southern California; very tan, streaked blond hair, a lot of makeup applied so skillfully that it looked like nearly none, and trendy clothes. She, too, was in a tennis outfit, but it was apparent she wasn't going to play anytime soon. Her right arm was in a cast from thumb to past her elbow. "How's it feeling?" Jane asked.

"Fine, so long as I don't try to use it. And I keep banging the cast into things."

"Shelley said you fell in the grocery store parking lot?"

"Yes, but not the grocery store down the street. I'd driven clear over to Oakview because somebody told me they had a good fish market. I never did find it, so I just ran into a strange store for a pack of cigarettes. I slipped on something as I came out. A nice man who was just behind me helped me up and took me to the emergency room of the community hospital."

Mary Ellen had put a cup and saucer in the dishwasher and pushed several buttons on a control panel that looked like part of NORAD as she spoke. Still using only her left hand, she was awkwardly rummaging in a recipe-card box. She tried to use her right hand to take out a card and winced.

"I always wanted a cast when I was a kid," Jane mused. "So people could write things on it. But I never broke a thing. I tried to make a cast once when my sister had some plaster of paris for a hobby project, but it just looked like I'd grown a limestone arm. My mother made me break it off and it took all the hair on my arm along with it. God, it hurts to remember."

Mary Ellen looked so pale that Jane was suddenly stricken with guilt. "Never mind the recipe. I shouldn't be bothering you."

"It's all right. Here it is," Mary Ellen said, handing her a card. "I think Shelley adds a little lemon juice and parsley to hers. Just don't lose the recipe card."

"Oh, I won't," Jane assured her, glad Shelley wasn't around to hear her making such a rash promise.

Mary Ellen walked to the door with her, and as they passed the den, Jane noticed that the computer was on and the screen was filled with some sort of graph. Mary Ellen had something to do with an investment group. Jane had never quite understood it or wanted to. All she knew was that it was extremely lucrative, and Mary Ellen did it at home most of the time, but had an office somewhere in Chicago where she went once every week or so. Steve had told her more, back when he'd been in his investment phase, but she hadn't been very interested. "So you can at least work?"

"What? Oh, yes. A little. Just with the one hand, though. It's very slow."

The phone began to ring. "Go ahead. I'll let myself out."

Jane hurried home, still half-afraid Shelley would catch her. Safely inside her own kitchen, she looked at the card and groaned.

Tangerine juice! Where the hell was she going to get tangerine juice?

Chapter Three

Jane was standing at the kitchen window, miserably contemplating where she'd find the elusive ingredient, when she heard Shelley's minivan pull back into the driveway between their houses. She must have taken the dog to the kennel and come back before going on to the airport. Thank heaven she hadn't been a minute earlier and caught Jane galloping across the street, waving a recipe card like a red flag.

Jane paced around a minute to see if Shelley would come right back out. Willard had inhaled his breakfast, and she shoved him out the back door into the fenced yard. He looked around cautiously to see if anyone was lurking there to get him. Willard, whose life's ambition was to escape into the front yard, was terrified of the back.

Going back in the kitchen, Jane found that the cats were still eyeing each other over their food bowl in a stare-off to determine who would eat first. "Get on with it, you dopes!" she said, giving them ear scritches they didn't appreciate.

Why didn't Shelley go? She didn't dare make a grocery-store run while there was a danger of Shelley catching her and asking where she was going. She found it was impossible to lie convincingly to her, even on small matters like tangerine juice. Jane would have to wait her out. It was like being in a castle under siege.

To kill the time, she occupied herself with one of her least favorite duties. She checked on the hamsters in Todd's room, which were living in precisely the kind of filth she'd imagined. "You are rats in disguise," she said to them. "You may fool children, but not mothers."

Popping the fuzzy creatures into a shoe box, she dumped the contents of their cage into a plastic trash bag—checking carefully just what she was throwing away. Once she'd tossed out their newborns not realizing what those repulsive little pink lumps were. She'd assumed they were evidence of some nasty digestive process she was better off not knowing anything about. Todd had been crushed, and had put no credence in Jane's statement that if he'd cleaned it himself as he was supposed to it wouldn't have happened. Sooner or later Todd would run out of friends to give the frequent offspring to, and they'd have to move out and abandon the house to the little rodents.

In the meantime, she'd keep cleaning their cage occasionally. She knew she shouldn't be doing this for Todd. It really was his responsibility. But there were reasons she continued to make regular forays into the hamster den. First, he was always so pleased when he came home and discovered that his little pals had a clean house. It was a refreshing change from the usual to have someone notice her efforts. Second, Steve had always been a bear about it, insisting that Jane was absolutely not to clean the cage. He didn't consider the creatures as pets, but as a learning experience for Todd. Now that he was gone, it was a backward sort of way to assert her independence.

Max and Meow had finished their breakfast and come upstairs to help her. They took up positions on either side of the shoe box and had their heads cocked alertly, listening to the hamsters scramble around. June had just put the hamsters back into their cage and was watching them burrow under the clean wood shavings when the phone rang. She shooed the cats out, slammed the door, and ran down to the kitchen to answer it so she could check on whether Shelley was gone. Her minivan was still in the drive as Jane lifted the receiver.

"Jane? You sound out of breath. There's not something wrong, is there?" a male voice rumbled.

"Hiya, Uncle Jim. Not a thing. What's up?"

"I'm calling about dinner Sunday—"

"You *are* coming, aren't you?"

"If you want me."

"That's a wimpy sort of thing for a macho cop to say. Of course I want you to come. If you didn't come every month, I'd be left to the mercy of Steve's mother and brother without any protection at all."

Uncle Jim, uncle in honorary terms only, asked, "Are they treating you all right, honey?"

"As all right as they know how. It's not their fault they drive me crazy."

"You're doing okay, then?"

"I'm fine, Uncle Jim. You haven't got around to why you're calling."

"Oh, just to warn you I might be a few minutes late. I've got to go out to the boys' detention home and take a statement from a kid who cut up his sister with a butcher knife."

"Don't try to kid me. You love nothing better than a nice hour of kicking ass at a detention home."

He laughed, then with mock-seriousness said, "Jane! What a way for a nice girl to talk."

Jane smiled to herself. To Uncle Jim she was still a girl. "You can't tell me a Chicago inner-city cop is shocked by my language."

"Honey, nothing shocks me anymore. Except maybe that cheese dip your mother-in-law made last time I came over."

"See you Sunday then."

As they concluded their conversation, Jane noticed Shelley get in her minivan and leave. She was looking ravishing in a rich, maroon suit with black piping and black patent accessories that were only slightly less shiny and neat than her hair.

The siege was lifted.

Jane changed from jeans and sweat shirt into tan culottes and a tan-and-white-striped sweater, took a quick swipe at her lips with a coral lipstick that Shelley had told her was her color, and headed for the closest grocery store. She got the carrots and onions, and for good measure picked up a wicked-looking paring knife, in the belief that any knife she might find in her kitchen would be too dull for the tricky business of cutting the onion as neatly as Shelley had specified. The last time she'd had a truly sharp knife Mike had used it to cut off a length of garden hose for a mysterious project. It was now good only for cutting butter—warm butter.

As she came down the dairy aisle, she spotted a plump, pimpled, and thoroughly harassed-looking young man with a tag that identified him as an assistant store manager. "Could you tell me where to find tangerine juice?" she asked.

"Tangerine juice?" He seemed deeply unhappy and slightly offended, as if she'd asked for amphetamines or hand grenades. "Have you checked the canned fruit juices?"

"Yes, mandarin orange and regular orange. No tangerine."

"Kool-Aid?"

"Nope. I looked."

"Jell-O?"

"I want to *flavor* a salad, not glue it together."

"Let's check the gourmet section, ma'am."

"This is proving a fruitless effort, in several senses," Jane giggled.

"You might try a health food store," he suggested, oblivious to her wit.

Jane shuddered. The only time she'd been in such an establishment, she'd seen only stuff that looked slightly less appetizing than the hamsters' food. "I don't frequent health food stores. I don't even know where one is."

In a low voice, as if afraid of being overheard giving information to the enemy, he gave her directions to a store several miles away.

Jane checked out and decided to do her other errands first. The health food store was the other way from her house. Smoking her second cigarette as she drove, she went to the bank, the office supply to pick up some graph paper Katie had requested, and to the dry cleaners to leave the sweater with the barbeque sauce on the sleeve. After a tiff with the girl at the desk, who insisted sourly that the stain looked like blood no matter what Jane might claim, she left.

She waited while a car pulled in next to hers. "Oh, hello, Jane," the woman getting out said.

"Robbie, you've done something to your hair. It looks nice."

Jane always went out of her way to compliment Robbie Jones, sensing that she needed it. Robbie was, to be generous, an extremely plain woman. She had a portly body and the skinniest arms and legs Jane had ever seen. In addition, she had a lantern jaw, low forehead, and a perpetually stern expression. But she had lovely auburn hair with a deep natural wave.

"I just had it trimmed a bit, that's all. Bringing in your dry cleaning?"

What else would I be doing at a dry cleaners? Jane wondered. Poor Robbie. She couldn't help it she was the world's worst conversationalist. Just shy, Jane supposed. Still, she often wondered how she did her job; Robbie worked part-time as a psychiatric nurse. A superb if boring organizer, she could handle work schedules and budgets with devastating competence, but she was the dreariest, most depressing person in their circle.

"You're coming to Shelley's this evening, aren't you?" she asked her.

"Certainly. I've got my food in the car to drop off in a while."

"I can take it for you, if you'd like."

"No, thank you. I've got my driving plan worked out and that would throw it completely off. I'll see you tonight."

Jane got in the car, biting back a smile. "I must learn to like her," she said out loud as she pulled out of the parking lot. "It's the Christian thing to do."

When she got home, she flipped on the kitchen television to catch the noon news while she fixed a sandwich and smoked another cigarette. Shelley might make fun of her meat loaf, but cold, it made the best sandwich in the world. The weather report caught her attention. A cold front was heading in their direction and would arrive later in the week. Temperatures might drop into the fifties or lower.

"Furnace—" she mumbled to herself. Every fall Steve did things to the furnace before it was turned on for the winter. But not this year. One more thing she'd have to figure out.

It was amazing how many things there were to learn when you were a single parent and a homeowner. There seemed to be hundreds of boring chores somebody else had always done and which had to be learned. What surprised her most was how many of them seemed to be seasonal. Every time she thought she had a grip on things, the weather changed, and she had to start all over with a whole new set of problems.

First it had been the snowblower. The rubber blades had worn down, and she and Mike had spent a hideous Saturday morning the previous February in a hardware store finding replacements. That was very soon after her world had caved in, and she'd made a fool of herself, breaking into tears, in public, when the hardware clerk told her how to have her husband attach the damned blades.

Then spring had come, and there'd been all the assorted jobs and implements associated with keeping a suburban yard looking decent. The lawn mower had been bad enough, but Mike had manfully assumed responsibility for it. Then the underground sprinkler system had suffered a breakdown that caused all but one of the heads to put out a pitiful mist and the remaining one to look like Old Faithful. That she'd just abandoned. She bought a rotating sprinkler head and a couple of lengths of hose. She'd always felt an underground sprinkling system was a symbol of decadence anyway. Spring had also meant having the snow tires taken off the station wagon, and she'd stupidly bought an entire new set of tires without realizing they weren't an annual purchase and the old ones were in green plastic bags in the basement.

When the weather had turned warm, the air conditioning had graciously consented to simply go on when she flipped the switch to "cool," and through some stroke of luck had worked all summer. But she was certain the furnace needed more than that. Something to do with the filter, she thought. Taking her last section of sandwich along, she went to the basement to look over the situation. She spent a useless half hour studying the thing and never found anything that faintly resembled a filter, but she did find a self-adhesive tag on the back of a little door that gave the name of the furnace repair company. Steve must have put it there.

Giving up, Jane went upstairs to make an appointment for the company to send a man out to look the thing over, then got to work on the carrot salad. She peeled and sliced the carrots with her new knife and put them into a steamer. While they cooked, she went out to hose off the patio. She had just turned off the water and was surveying her work with a sense of accomplishment when she heard a car door. Dear God—Shelley back? She glanced at her watch. One o'clock. It couldn't be. She peered around the corner through the hedge that ran all the way from her house to Shelley's and saw Joyce Greenway approaching Shelley's kitchen door.

"She's not home," Jane called out.

Joyce peered into the shrubbery, trying to spot the source of the voice. "I know. She told me. Could you get the door? I'm about to drop this thing." Joyce was tiny— barely five feet and probably not over ninety-five pounds, all of it in exactly the right places. She had curly, silky-fine blond hair, and a very soft voice which hardly ever seemed to rise much above a whisper, but which she managed to project superbly. She'd been a professional actress for a few years and was still active in community theater. Jane supposed that's where she'd honed the skill of being heard.

Jane went in through her garage and back out into the adjoining driveways. She opened Shelley's kitchen door and followed Joyce inside. "What've you got?"

"Brisket. I'm not sure it's well enough done, but I was afraid to wait. Shelley's such a terror about getting the food over early. What did you make?"

"Carrot salad—oh, Lord!—I forgot, the carrots are cooking! Gotta run. Can you find a place in the refrigerator for that?" Jane didn't wait for a reply. She was relieved to have a legitimate excuse to escape. Joyce was very nice, but awfully solicitous of Jane's single state—always asking how the children were doing without their father and was there anything she could do to help out. It got a bit tiresome.

The water under the carrots had reduced itself to a mere skin on the bottom of the pan, but nothing had started to burn yet. Jane speared a carrot slice to see if it was done, and it practically dissolved under the assault. Damn it, she'd have to start over. This stuff would turn to carrot paste if she tried to stir it. Good thing she'd got plenty of carrots.

This time she stood by the stove and turned the kitchen timer on for good measure. She spread the morning paper out and browsed through, but found nothing of earthshaking interest. Least of all ads for sales on tangerine juice. She paced, wishing the carrots would hurry up. She still had to find the last ingredient and put the salad together before Shelley got home and discovered her lapse. Finally, the timer went off. She jerked the pot off the burner, dumped the carrots into a bowl, and set it in the refrigerator. Time to find the health food store.

Yet another cook was arriving next door and, thinking it would be surly to ignore her—they'd had words once when Mike and her Eddie were in third grade about the room-mother assignments, and Jane was still feeling the need to mend fences—she stopped and said, "Hi, Laura."

Laura Stapler nearly threw her dish in the air. "Oh, Jane! I didn't see you. You shouldn't sneak up on people like that!"

"Sorry. Shelley's not home, but you can go on in."

"I know. She called and told me she'd be out. Doesn't she lock up the house when she leaves?"

This question from Laura wasn't surprising. She was a timid, mousy woman who always looked like she had inside information that the world was about to end and was under orders not to tell anyone. Her husband had a franchised "safety store" in the nearest shopping mall. He had a tendency to bring his work home. Their house, which Jane had visited once, was locked up like an Egyptian tomb. They had dead bolts, alarm wires, and even a padlock on the side gate. "I'll bet she wears a chastity belt that's hooked up to the alarm system," Joyce had once said. To which Shelley replied with a malicious grin, "I've met her husband—I don't imagine the alarm goes off very often!"

"There's someone there, Laura. The cleaning lady," Jane reassured her, thinking Laura would be afraid to even set foot in a house that wasn't properly secure.

"Oh, I'm *so* glad!" Laura said.

Jane found the health food store with difficulty. It was located, as she felt only proper, around the side of a line of shops, almost entirely out of sight. The clerk, a man of enormous proportions, tugged at his skimpy beard and said, "Tangerine juice? Naw. We got peach nectar and unstrained apple juice and apricot nectar and unsweetened grapefruit juice and pressed carrot essence and some heart of celery cocktail—no liquor, of course. I think we've maybe got some plum nectar. You wouldn't like that, would you?"

"Definitely not."

Even though she needed to hurry, Jane couldn't resist looking around a bit. Everything, she discovered quickly, was brown. Light brown and dark brown, pinkish brown or greenish brown. She glanced back at the clerk, now trying to squeeze his way along behind the counter, and wondered how in the world he had got that shape eating only the kind of stuff sold in the store. Maybe brown was a fattening color. That, she mused, might make a best-selling diet book. *The NonBrown Way to Beauty*.

Musing about food colors, Jane returned to the car. Could you eat only red food? Rare steak, candied apples, new potatoes in their pink skins, cranberry juice, strawberry pie—she'd have to fix all that sometime and see how it looked. What about green? Okay for the vegetables, and some sort of mint dessert, but she couldn't think of a green meat, except some she had accidentally turned that shade in the refrigerator from time to time.

She was passing a grocery story she'd never been in and decided it couldn't hurt to try. If she didn't find the tangerine juice there, she'd have to give up and use orange juice and just face Shelley's wrath. She turned back at the next corner, parked, and went in. With a panicked glance at her watch, she headed straight for the office booth next to the check-out stands. After waiting impatiently for a moment, she asked the young woman operating an adding machine if they carried tangerine juice.

Without looking up, she replied, "We're out, ma'am, but we have an order coming in Monday."

"I beg your pardon? You mean you actually carry it?"

"Oh, sure. There might be a can that got mixed up with something else, if you want to look. Frozen concentrates."

Fortunately, this guess turned out to be right. Clutching the frigid can as if it were solid gold, Jane paid and hurried out to the car. Time was running short if she was going to have the salad waiting at Shelley's when she got home from lunching with her mother at the airport. It was 2:15 when she got home, and 2:45 by the time she'd finished the business of slicing the onions paper-thin as ordered while fending off several annoying phone calls from people who wanted to sell her roofing and siding and thermal windows.

Finally, triumphantly bearing the bowl of carrot salad, she hurried across the two driveways and into Shelley's kitchen. She was home free; if Shelley came in now, she'd claim the salad had been there for hours and she'd just come in to check that the rest of the dishes had arrived. For the sake of backing up this story, if necessary, Jane looked around. The refrigerator's middle shelf contained three other bowls of salad, and the platter of sliced brisket she'd seen Joyce bring. Apparently nothing had interfered with Robbie Jones's driving schedule, because there was also a bowl of vegetable dip and a Tupperware container on the counter full of the butter-soaked, baked wheat-bread fingers that she always brought to this sort of thing. Next to this was the sheet cake.

Jane was tempted to just nibble one of the wheat-bread goodies, but was afraid either Shelley or the cleaning lady would catch her at it. Besides, Robbie probably knew exactly how many she'd brought and would take roll call of them later. Jane went home instead, and cleaned up the mess she'd made fixing the carrot salad. A few minutes later she heard Shelley's minivan, and five minutes after that the phone rang again.

"Jane—?"

"Shelley? Is that you?"

"Jane, come over!"

"In a few minutes, Shelley. I just dropped a peanut butter jar and there's glass all over—"

"Jane, shut up! Come over. The cleaning lady's dead. Do you hear me, Jane? She's dead! In my guest bedroom!"

Chapter Four

In all the years they'd been friends, Jane had never known Shelley to lose her cool. But on the phone she'd been shrill, nearly hysterical. As Jane raced across the driveways and into the Nowack's kitchen door, Shelley met her, wringing her hands and looking like death. Her face could have been painted white.

"I can't have heard you right," Jane panted.

"She's dead, Jane. It's horrible."

"Did you call the police and an ambulance?"

"Not yet. An ambulance won't help her."

"You don't know that, Shelley. It might be a heart attack or something. Maybe she just looks dead."

"Jane, believe me—" Shelley turned away and put her hand over her mouth, retching.

Jane ran up the stairs, skidding to a halt just inside the door to the guest room. She suddenly realized what Shelley meant. The cleaning lady was lying sprawled beside the bed, just inside the doorway. Feet toward the door, face down, her head was turned sideways, and what Jane could see was sickening. The woman's skin was a mottled purple, her eyes bulged, and something fat and purplish and repulsive was sticking out of her mouth. It took Jane a few seconds to realize it was the woman's tongue.

The vacuum cleaner cord was twisted savagely around her bruised throat.

Jane's stomach heaved and she dashed for the bathroom. She clung to the sink, steeling herself. Then she rinsed her mouth, slapped some cold water on her face, and—carefully not looking toward the guest room—started downstairs. She had to lean on the banister for support. Her knees were shaking so badly she nearly tumbled forward twice.

Shelley was at the bottom of the stairs, and they fell into each other's arms. "Oh, my God, Shelley—" Jane whimpered. Shelley was crying. "We have to call the police. They'll take care of—of everything." She knew she was babbling, but she needed to say something.

"Oh, Jane . . ." Shelley moaned. "Take care of it? This is too awful. How could something so terrible happen?"

"That's for the police to figure out," Jane said. Since the normally bossy Shelley was on the verge of going to pieces, Jane felt the need to be confident. But her voice came out in a croaking manner that didn't sound like herself.

"Yes. Yes, you're right. I'll call," Shelley said, wiping her eyes on the sleeve of her elegant maroon suit. In other circumstances, Jane would have fainted from astonishment at seeing such a thing. Of course, in other circumstances, Shelley would never have done that.

"What shall I say?"

"I don't know," Jane said, following her back to the kitchen. They were moving along like children, clinging to each other as if afraid to let go.

Shelley picked up the phone, then put it back down. "I can't hear with that dishwasher going," she said. She looked down at the little light indicating the cycle. She went even whiter than before. "It's just on prewash . . ." she said tonelessly.

"So what? Just cancel the cycle— My God, Shelley!" Jane said, suddenly realizing the implications of this. "Did you start it before you found her?"

"No, she"—she gestured helplessly toward the stairs— "must have."

"Then that means she's only been dead a few minutes. Whoever did it might still be here."

They looked toward the family room, and suddenly the chairs and sofas became menacing—hiding places where murderers might be lurking. Jane grabbed Shelley's arm. "We'll call from my house."

"We shouldn't leave her. It doesn't seem decent."

"Decent! Nothing about this is decent, Shelley. Anyway, we can't do her any good now."

Holding hands like terrified schoolgirls, they ran across the adjoining drives and into Jane's kitchen. Willard greeted them, then ran for cover, sensing that something was very wrong. After misdialing twice, Shelley finally managed to convey to the police that someone had been murdered in her house and that she was safely waiting at her neighbor's house. She gave her address and Jane's, and was barely through talking when the faint wail of a siren sounded on the main thoroughfare a few blocks over.

They stood looking at each other. "What do I do now?" Shelley asked.

"Nothing. Just wait. Want a cigarette?"

Shelley had quit nearly a year before, but accepted the offer with gratitude. "You'll stay with me, won't you?" she said, coughing a little as she took the first drag.

"Yes, of course. I've got to take care of car pools." In spite of the situation, the mother part of Jane was still working, consulting a mental file cabinet of everyday responsibilities. "Mike will get himself home, and Katie is supposed to be staying for a pep rally and coming home with a friend. but Todd—"

Keeping an eye on Shelley, who looked shaky, she picked up the phone, thought for a minute, then dialed Dorothy Wallenberg's number.

"Dorothy! Thank goodness you're home. I need a couple favors. Something awful has happened. Shelley's cleaning lady has—has died. Yes, it's terrible. Yes, just now. I'll tell her you said that. Just at the moment, *I'm* the one who needs some help. Please, would you pick up Todd for me and take him home with you? And call everybody who's supposed to be coming tonight to the meeting at Shelley's house and tell them it's been cancelled. No, I'm not sure—"

She glanced at Shelley, who had balanced the cigarette on the edge of the table and was leaning over with her head between her knees, breathing deeply. "I can't ask her, Dorothy. Just call anybody you think might have been coming. I think Laura Stapler has a list of the committee members. Start with her. Thanks, Dorothy."

Shelley stood up and went to the window, swaying slightly. The wail of the first siren stopped abruptly, and through Jane's kitchen window they could see that there was one officer sprinting around the far side of Shelley's house and another coming around the near corner. They had their guns drawn. Another, having apparently parked on the next street, vaulted nimbly over the back fence and headed, crouching, toward the basement door that opened out of the back of the house. Jane could hear at least two other sirens. "Dorothy says if there's anything you need or want, just call her."

Shelley turned away from the window, sat down, and pushed her hair back from her face. "That's nice of her," she said with mechanical courtesy.

Jane's phone rang and she answered curtly. "Yes?"

"Jane! This is Mary Ellen. I just looked out the front window. What's wrong at Shelley's?"

"The cleaning lady's been killed. The killer may still be in the house."

"Edith? Killed?"

"Yes—no, not Edith. It was a substitute. Somebody strangled her."

"Oh, my God," Mary Ellen said, sounding nearly as bad as Shelley did. "What can I do? Is Shelley all right?"

"She's not hurt. You can't do anything. Just stay in the house until it's over. I'll talk to you later."

Shelley was rummaging in the cabinet for Jane's jar of instant coffee. Meow jumped onto the counter to see what was going on that might provide nibbles for her. There was no sign of Willard. Probably hiding in the basement. Hands shaking, Jane turned on a burner and started some water boiling. They didn't speak. Jane had a strange nightmarish sense of reality and horror interwoven. Next door, a dead woman lay in the guest bedroom and police searched the house. Here, they were silently making coffee, as if that were a solution to something.

Shelley sat trembling at the table, sipping her coffee. Jane watched out the window. More emergency vehicles arrived, and somebody put up white-and-orange-striped sawhorses several doors down to stop traffic. Dear God, it would scare the kids to death if they came home and found the neighborhood seemingly under martial law. Todd would be at Dorothy's house, but Mike and Katie . . .

Hating to do it, Jane picked up the phone again and called her mother-in-law. "Thelma? Jane. I can only talk a second. Something awful has happened next door and the police have the block cordoned off. No, I'm fine. I'm not in any danger. But I'm worried about Mike and Katie trying to come home and thinking something has happened to me. I can't get out. Would you please call their schools and order them to stay there until you or Ted can pick them up? Thanks, Thelma. I'll come over to get them just as soon as I can."

As she hung up, there was a knock on the front door. Opening it gingerly, she was faced with a cop who couldn't have been more than twenty. "Is the homeowner of the house next door here? I was given this address."

"Yes, please come in."

She introduced herself and Shelley and he said, "We've gone through the house, and there's nobody there but the victim. We'll need to ask you some questions. Would you rather stay here for a while to answer them?"

"Yes, I would," Shelley said. She'd gotten a grip on herself and was back to her normal color. "I think Mrs. Jeffry can probably tell you more than I can anyway. I've been gone almost all day. You were home, weren't you, Jane?"

"Mostly. I ran some errands. Tangerine juice," she added.

"Why didn't you just take some out of my freezer?" Shelley asked.

"Do you mean I ran all over town and it was next door all the time?" She felt an urge to laugh, but knew it would turn into full-blown hysteria if she started.

Another officer had come to the kitchen door, and with him there was a handsome, blond man in a business suit who introduced himself as Detective Mel VanDyne. He looked like a movie version of an investigator—shoulders wide enough to slightly strain an expensively tailored jacket, and smooth, economical gestures. As soon as Shelley and Jane identified themselves, he said in a deep, reassuring voice, "I noticed the uniform the victim was wearing and I've called the company to send someone over to make the identification, Mrs. Nowack."

"Thank you. I couldn't look at her again," Shelley said, lighting another cigarette, then stubbing it out. "I shouldn't be doing this. I quit."

"You'll quit again tomorrow," Detective VanDyne said in a voice so assured that Jane felt certain it would happen just as he said. "Do you have any idea what happened?"

"None. I left around— Oh, dear, I don't really remember—"

"It was ten o'clock. I saw you go," Jane put in.

"Where did you go?"

"To the airport. To have lunch with my mother. I've been there the whole time. I'm sure there are people at the restaurant who will remember us. My mother managed to offend nearly every employee—"

Detective VanDyne's smile was friendly. "I wasn't asking you for an alibi, yet. But thanks anyway. When did you get back?"

Shelley didn't even bother to answer. She looked at Jane.

"At three, or a few minutes before. I was at her house at quarter of and she wasn't back yet."

VanDyne gazed at Jane speculatively. "What were you doing there?"

"Taking over a carrot salad."

"I'm having—I *was* having a meeting at my house tonight. A group that's planning to raise funds for new playground equipment," Shelley explained. "It was a pot-luck dinner, and everybody was supposed to bring their food ahead of time."

"So you were letting people in for Mrs. Nowack?" the detective asked Jane.

"No, I just left the door unlocked," Shelley said. "It's not as if the house were empty."

VanDyne shook his head disapprovingly. "Can you give me a list of the people who came over?" He addressed this question to the air halfway between them.

Shelley's voice was a shade haughty. "You don't mean to suggest that one of my friends killed the woman?"

"Ma'am, I haven't any idea who did it. Not yet. But I

must obviously begin with the people who were known to be there."

"It doesn't matter," Jane said. "She was only killed a few minutes before we called you. Only moments before Shelley came home."

"If you don't think it's impertinent of me to ask, how do you know that?"

"Because the dishwasher was on the prewash cycle when Shelley got home and discovered the body." She glanced at Shelley for confirmation, but Shelley had gotten dangerously pale and was carefully pouring herself more coffee with shaking hands. Jane went on. "That means the cleaning lady must have started it between the time I was there and the time Shelley got home. Everybody had already brought their food and gone when I went over at quarter to three."

"Still, I need the names of the people who were there and when."

"Oh, all right. Let me think. Dorothy Wallenberg brought a sheet cake early in the morning."

"A sheet cake?"

"You know, the kind that's done in a big, flat pan. You don't have to ice the sides or worry about it not rising evenly or—"

VanDyne wasn't interested in the fine points of baking for a meeting. "Did this Wallenberg woman know Mrs. Nowack wasn't at home?"

"I was home then," Shelley said. "But Jane brought the cake in for her."

"I see. Go on, Mrs. Jeffry."

"Let's see. Joyce Greenway brought a brisket over about one o'clock. And Laura Stapler came with a cucumber and onion salad around twenty minutes later. However long it took me to cook the carrots—for my salad, you see."

"Who else?" Detective VanDyne asked, not to be sidetracked with carrot cooking time.

"Robbie Jones brought some dip and this wonderful crunchy thing she makes—whole wheat fingers."

The detective's eyebrows shot up, but he resisted. "When was that?"

"I don't know. I didn't see her."

"Then how do you know she brought them?"

"Well, they're there. They didn't just materialize," Jane snapped. These quibbling interruptions were irritating.

"No, I mean, how do you know *she* brought them, and not somebody else?"

"She always does. And the dip was in her funny, discolored Tupperware bowl. I always think I could get the stain out if I could get my hands on it. I had one like that, and soaked it overnight in—"

"Mrs. Jeffry!"

"Yes. I guess that is beside the point. But you asked."

"All right. Assuming you can tell who was there by the food, who else had been there?"

"Well, there was a pasta salad I didn't recognize. Everybody's making pasta salads these days."

"That was Suzie Williams," Shelley put in. "She lives next door on the other side of me. She called and told me she was anxious to try out a new recipe."

"And there was a potato salad in a huge orange ceramic bowl with white flecks," Jane added. "I've seen it before. Who does that belong to, Shelley?"

"Mary Ellen Revere."

"Of course. She lives across the street."

"Is that it?"

Jane could see out the window. "Yes . . ." she said slowly as she watched a gurney with a covered shape being wheeled out to the ambulance. A man in coveralls the same blue as the cleaning lady's pant suit was walking alongside.

Jane suddenly felt sick again, but it had nothing to do with the murder victim. She was thinking of Steve. He must have been taken away like that, his face covered. But it had been the middle of the night, freezing and snowing. And instead of lush, green lawn, there must have been only twisted metal, bent guardrails, ice-coated pavement, and blood everywhere. Steve's blood and the truck driver's, probably steaming in the frigid night air at first, then crystallizing on the snow.

And he'd had nobody to walk beside him.

Chapter Five

"Mrs. Jeffry, could you give me addresses for the women you've mentioned? I'll have to contact them."

"What—? Oh, yes, of course." Jane dragged herself back to the present. What was going on now was bad enough; the past was unthinkable. She got her address book out from the drawer beneath the phone and started recording the information on a notepad.

"I'll take you home anytime you're ready, Mrs. Nowack," Detective VanDyne was saying. "Do you need anyone called? Your husband—?"

"No, he's out of town. So are my children. I'll phone him later this afternoon when things—when I've calmed down. Uh—about that room—the guest room—?"

"It's all right. Death is sometimes very messy. This one wasn't," he said, correctly interpreting her concern. "Of course, we've got a photographer and a fingerprint man there still, but they'll clean up after themselves—in their fashion—when they're done. We'll have to take the vacuum cleaner to the lab for a few days to try to get some prints off the cord. It's unlikely they'll find any full prints, though. Is there anything else you can tell me about all this? What do you know about Mrs. Thurgood?"

"Mrs. Thurgood? Who's that?"

He looked at her with some alarm. "Mrs. Thurgood is the woman who was murdered."

"Oh, I'm so sorry. I didn't know that was her name. I suppose she must have told me, but—"

"She worked for you every week and you didn't know her name?"

"No. I'd never had her to my house before. She was a substitute for the woman the agency was supposed to send."

"I didn't know that," Detective VanDyne said.

"Does it matter?" Jane asked, looking up from her task of compiling names and addresses.

"Who can say?" he answered. "I don't know anything yet." He turned back to Shelley. "Are you ready to go home?"

"I'll come with you, Shelley," Jane said. She handed the list to the detective and wondered if he'd be able to read her handwriting. She hardly recognized it as her own.

"No, Jane. I'm fine now. Really. Go get your kids back from the Dragon Lady."

Jane smiled. "Okay. But you'll come over for dinner?"

Shelley agreed and went off with her protector. Jane called her mother-in-law and made the briefest possible explanation of what had occurred. "I'll be over in a few minutes to pick up the kids."

"Oh, no need, Jane. They're happy as clams here. I've fixed a nice angel food cake. I know how Mike loves them."

"And I suppose he's wolfing it down now and spoiling his appetite for dinner?" This was one of Thelma's favorite tricks. She used to do it all the time with Steve, asking him to stop by to visit her in the late afternoon for some reason, then filling him up so he wouldn't want whatever Jane had fixed.

"Oh, were you cooking dinner tonight? I had no idea," Thelma said with a little laugh.

"I always cook dinner," Jane lied. She eyed a Kentucky Fried Chicken box from the evening before in the waste-basket. *I must not lose my temper with her*, she told herself. *She's doing me a favor at the moment and that puts her in a position of power.* "I'll be over in a few minutes."

She then reported in to Dorothy Wallenberg. "I'm running over to pick up Todd. I appreciate your helping me out."

"Jane, what in heaven's name happened at Shelley's?"

"The cleaning lady was murdered."

"Murdered! My God! You said before that she died. I thought a heart attack or something. Murdered? Who did it?"

"Nobody knows. Please, Dorothy, don't tell Todd about it being murder yet. I want to sort of ease into it with him later. Without any warning, it would scare him to death."

"Of course it would. It scares me, and I'm worried about you being right next door. Shelley's home alone right now, too, isn't she? Thank God her children were gone. Don't worry about getting Todd. He's out playing with the kids, and I'd promised to take them all out for Burger King. Let me just bring him back to you later."

"Thanks, Dorothy. That sounds wonderful. The police ought to be gone by then and it'll be less horrible."

As she backed out to go get Mike and Katie, the last police car pulled away. All that remained was a red MG. That had to be Detective VanDyne's. Somehow he looked like the sort of bachelor who'd have one.

When Jane got to her mother-in-law's, Thelma was greedy for details about the crisis. She was a stately, angular, blue-haired lady with a perpetually haughty look, but her usual frosty manner thawed as she exclaimed, "Murder! Good Lord, Jane. How terrible! Well, it just goes to prove what I've always said—you and the children ought to move in here with me. It's not safe for you to be living alone."

Jane gritted her teeth and took a deep breath. "Thelma, you'd have hardly been able to prevent this, and none of us were endangered anyway." This, she knew, was beside the point. Her mother-in-law had been harping for months on how they ought to move in with her. The bedrooms in her elegant condo were the size of skating rinks, but there were only two of them, and Jane sometimes had nightmares about living there and having to be Thelma's "roommate." Of course, Thelma didn't really want them there; what she was really angling for was an invitation to move in with them.

"She'd be packed in thirty seconds," Jane had said to Shelley the week before, "if I even hinted that I might agree. It would be like having General Patton around the house. Slapping the troops—namely me—for their own good."

"You've got to stand firm, Jane," Shelley had advised.

"She'd have you asking her permission to pee within the week."

"It's this modern permissive society," Thelma was going on. "When standards are allowed to slip, we're all in peril."

"I can't see how that figures, Thelma. We don't even know anything about this woman or why she was killed."

"Mark my words, it'll all come out eventually and you'll see I'm right. Ah, children, your mother has finally come to pick you up," she said as Mike and Katie came out of the second bedroom, which was fitted out as a TV room. Thelma had every video game in the world, part of her insidious campaign to make herself indispensable. She managed, too, by some mysterious process that Jane found highly suspicious, to get rental movies before they were even in the rental shops.

"What's goin' on, Mom?" Mike asked.

"Mother! I was supposed to go to Jenny's after school and Gram said you wouldn't let me," Katie complained.

Jane cast a black look at Thelma, who was smiling fondly on her grandchildren.

"I'll explain on the way home. Get your things," Jane said. "Thelma, I don't know how to thank you for your support."

"It's the least I can do, Jane. After all, they *are* my own flesh and blood."

As she drove home ("No, Mike, my nerves are too frayed to ride with you in rush-hour traffic."), she explained to them what had happened in the most innocuous way she could. Her aim was to make the murder sound like a pure freak of nature that would almost instantly be sorted out, with no danger to them whatsoever. But in her own mind she was deeply troubled. If somebody could commit murder in Shelley's house, they could do it in hers. The first thing she was going to do when she got home was check all the locks.

The kids, however, weren't upset. They were fascinated by the idea of a real live murder next door. To them, it was an adventure, impersonal and exciting, like something on television. Tomorrow they'd be the center of attention at school, famous for their proximity to something so out of the ordinary. They hadn't known the victim, so they had no sense of personal loss. Nor had they had the misfortune of actually viewing death, as Jane had. Best of all, they showed no signs of making any connection with their father. They'd grieved him properly at the time, and still missed him, but this didn't appear to be reactivating their distress, as it had with her.

They're so damned resilient, Jane thought. *It must come from having no sense of their own mortality yet.*

Shelley came to dinner, and in front of the kids neither she nor Jane discussed the afternoon's events. Todd turned up, filled to the brim with a double cheese Whopper and fries and content to listen to Mike and Katie's account without taking much interest. Eventually they all wandered off to their separate pursuits, and Jane and Shelley were left to sit over the remnants of the makeshift dinner.

"You'll stay here tonight?" Jane said. It was halfway between an invitation and an order.

"Thanks, I'm planning to. Mary Ellen Revere invited me to stay at her house and I lied and said I'd already agreed to stay here. I know I've got to get it over with, sleeping in that house, but not until Paul gets back tomorrow. He tried to get a flight tonight and couldn't. I called my sister and told her that, if this isn't solved by the time they're ready to come back, I want her to keep the kids a little longer. Jane, why do you suppose this happened?"

"I have no idea. I guess it could have been someone that woman knew."

"But why? And how would the killer have known she was at my house? As I understand it, *she* didn't even know where she'd be until she reported in to work early this morning. The Happy Helper man called a while ago. He said she's a 'floater,' a worker with no regular assignment but to fill in. Like a substitute teacher."

"Well, there's always the wandering maniac theory. That's what Thelma thinks—somebody whose lack of moral fiber pushed them over the brink."

"The next stage after growing hair on the palms of your hands? Murdering cleaning ladies? Forget wandering maniacs. You know as well as I do this is a neighborhood of devoted snoops. You can't even go for a walk without somebody alerting the police. If you aren't decked out like a full-fledged jogger, you're assumed to be a criminal. How would this maniac have cruised around the neighborhood without being noticed?"

"You know what you're saying, don't you? That it had to be someone familiar. Someone from the neighborhood."

Shelley's eyes widened. "Not necessarily, Jane. It could have been someone who looked like they had business around here. A TV repair truck or a Sears van or a gas meter reader in a uniform."

"Shelley, what would be the point? There would be no reason to go to all the trouble of disguising himself just to kill her in your house instead of her own."

"There is that, of course. Well, then we have to consider that he didn't want to kill her. Suppose it was someone who came to rob the house."

"Was anything stolen?"

"No, nothing was touched, apparently. I haven't searched everything, of course, but it doesn't look like anything's been torn apart or dumped out, as if someone had been rummaging for valuables."

Jane had to take her word on this. If you moved so much as an ashtray in Shelley's house, she noticed immediately.

"So why kill her and not take anything?"

"Maybe she caught him coming in?"

"While she was vacuuming the guest room?"

"Jane, you're just picking apart everything I suggest as a possibility," Shelley said with a hint of anger. "What do you think could have happened?"

"I'm sorry. I don't know. But, by damn, I'm going to find out. We're all in danger until we know who it was and why. If someone could come in your house, murder someone, and leave right under our noses, it could happen again."

"But why would it happen again? Why did it happen this time? I just keep asking myself the same questions over and over."

"All right. Let's get organized about this. I read a lot of mystery books and I know all about motives. I'll make a list and then we'll cross them off one by one. Whichever one's left has to be the right answer."

"Somehow, I don't think it's quite that easy," Shelley disagreed. You make it sound like a computer course."

"You'll see," Jane assured her, getting out the notepad and a stub of pencil. "Since it didn't look like robbery, let's assume for the moment that somebody meant to kill her. Now, what are the reasons for murder. Greed. That's usual."

"I doubt that a cleaning lady had a vast fortune for someone to inherit, otherwise she'd own the company. And she didn't seem to be wearing a strand of emeralds or anything that I noticed."

"True, but it might have been greed for something in your house."

"But I told you, nothing was taken."

"Still, it might have been that the murderer *meant* to take something and just didn't get it. Suppose he'd gone in and determined to kill anybody who was there and then rob the place, and just as he killed her, he heard you coming in?"

She was immediately sorry she'd suggested it.

Shelley hugged herself. "Could I have actually been in the house with the killer? No, Jane. That doesn't work. If he didn't mind killing her, he wouldn't have minded killing me. And how would he have gotten away? If he'd jumped from a second-story window, he'd have been bound to hurt himself, and the police checked all around the house for signs of things like that. If he didn't go out the window, he'd had to have come downstairs, and I could see the stairway from the time I came in the kitchen. I wasn't looking at it, but I would have certainly noticed anyone coming down."

"Okay, cross off greed. It was just a suggestion. Reasons for murder. Greed, fear—"

"Fear of what? That woman? Would you be afraid of her?"

"Not physically. But what if she knew something the killer was afraid she'd tell?"

"Jane, you met that woman. She didn't strike me as knowing how to tell time, much less dangerous secrets.

Besides, the question I asked earlier applies—why kill her at my house? Why not at her own, or on the street?"

"I don't know about the *where*-to-kill-her part, but think some more about the *why*. Just suppose that she'd been cleaning some office, though. You said she was a substitute and went all sorts of places. Suppose she learned something about a company take-over, or—"

"Happy Helpers doesn't do businesses. Only domestic jobs. I tried to get them for Paul's office."

"Some people do their business at home. Mary Ellen Revere, for instance."

"With a broken arm she can't even use? She strangles her?"

"Of course not. I didn't mean her. I was just making an example of somebody around here who has a business at home." Jane sighed. "Now who's shooting down ideas? All right. Cross off fear. What else is a motive for murder? Well, there's mercy killing, but this obviously wasn't a method of putting a loved one out of her misery. What about revenge?"

The phone rang and Jane answered somewhat impatiently. It was Laura Stapler, inviting Shelley and her and the kids to spend the night at their house. Jane had a momentary vision of being cooped up in the Stapler's house like survivors of a nuclear attack. "That's sweet of you, Laura, but Shelley's staying here and I think we'll be fine."

"You do have the house locked up tightly, don't you? And be sure to draw the blinds. My husband could put a rush order through and have an alarm system installed for you tomorrow if you'd like. Normally it takes a week or so, but under the circumstances—"

"That's very thoughtful, but I really can't afford it."

"We could arrange for financing, thirty six months at fifteen percent."

"Laura, no, thank you!" Jane said firmly.

Sensing she'd gone too far or in the wrong direction, Laura tried to reemphasize her concern for Jane's safety without selling anything. Jane hung up after listening long enough to convince Laura that she wasn't offended. "What ghouls! Where were we? Oh, yes, revenge."

"For what?"

"Who knows? Maybe Mrs. Thurgood did some awful thing to somebody and they got back at her by strangling her."

Shelley tapped her immaculately manicured fingernails on the table, considering. "It's certainly possible. Without knowing anything about her, there's no reason to mark it off the motive list, but my instincts tell me otherwise."

"I know what you mean. Somehow she seemed too—too bland to have ever done something awful."

The phone rang and Jane answered, afraid that Laura had thought of another safety device to peddle. A can of Mace or something. But it was Detective VanDyne. She handed the phone to Shelley and cleaned up the dinner table while Shelley talked—or rather, listened. Except for the occasional "uh-huh" or "I see," it would have seemed she was on hold.

Finally, she hung up and came back to the table. Jane poured them each coffee from a fresh pot. It was after eight, so she'd switched over to decaf.

"He wants to leave a man in the house overnight."

"Why?"

"Well, he didn't say so in so many words, but the gist of it was that he has absolutely no motives or suspects yet."

"Greed, fear, mercy, revenge? Nothing?" She wondered why, with so many motives available, he hadn't found one he liked.

"No, he told me he'd spent the evening interviewing her coworkers. It seems she's a childless widow who's only lived in the area for two months and has been on welfare most of that time. Some private agency for indigent widows. Before she came here, she drove a paper route in a little farm community in Montana and taught Sunday school."

"Nobody would want or need to kill somebody like that," Jane said.

"But somebody did," Shelley reminded her.

Chapter Six

Jane hardly slept all night. Dreams of vacuum cleaners run amok and red MGs coming out of dishwashers haunted her. At one point, a vacuum cleaner cord turned into a boa constrictor and wound itself around her. An army of identical women in blue uniforms marched in the house and changed everything and it wasn't her house anymore. When she woke before the alarm, sweating and exhausted, she could smell coffee. Shelley was already in the kitchen, puttering around silently. She had on faded jeans and a baggy pink cotton shirt that was wrinkled just enough to be trendy without looking sloppy. But for the first time Jane could remember, her friend looked tired and worried.

"Paul called from the airport," she said as she poured Jane a cup of coffee.

"I didn't hear the phone." Apparently she'd slept more soundly than she realized.

"I got it on the first ring. He got some sort of middle-of-the-night milk flight and is on his way now, after about sixteen stopovers."

"You don't have to go to the airport, do you?"

"No, he left a company car there."

Jane took a cautious sip. Shelley's coffee had a reputation for burning the bottom out of cups. Steve used to say you had to use a blowtorch to cool it. But this time it wasn't bad. Jane dragged out a package of grocery-store donuts and offered Shelley one. They sat together in companionable silence for a few minutes, and finally Shelley sighed and brushed the donut crumbs into a neat pile in the center of her paper napkin. "So, what are you doing today?"

"Whatever you need me to do."

"I don't think I need anything, but that's sweet of you. It's all over now, or at least I hope to God it is. Don't you drive your blind children this morning?"

One of Jane's volunteer activities was to take a group of blind children from the high school to a weekly session in special techniques in daily living. "Not until Friday."

"This *is* Friday."

"No! It is! I was supposed to have Edith to clean for the first time today. Oh, Lord! I haven't even straightened up enough for her to work on the actual dirt. Do you think they'll send her, after what happened?"

"I can't imagine why not."

Jane was already scurrying around the kitchen, throwing things in the dishwasher and wastebasket with random abandon. Out of the corner of her eye, she noticed a car coming down the street. Shelley was instantly on the move.

"There's Paul," she said, slipping on her immaculate tennis shoes.

"Get along, then. I'll check with you later and see if there's anything you need."

Jane went through the house like a demented whirlwind. Steve used to have a fit about Jane's feeling that she had to tidy up for the cleaning lady's arrival. "That's what you're paying her to do," he'd say as she snatched the newspaper away from him to dispose of it the moment he was through.

"Men just don't understand. I'm paying her to do the *real* cleaning, the stuff I hate," she'd explained repeatedly. "The icky corners of the bathroom, the windowsill dusting, the serious clear-to-the-corner vacuuming, scrubbing the stains out of the sink. But a cleaning lady can't get to that unless everything is picked up."

As she passed the door to her bedroom, she heard her alarm buzzing and realized she'd forgotten the time in her frantic haste to prepare for Edith. She roused the boys without much sympathy for their sleepy pleas for another five minutes. Katie was already up, doing her hair. "Put away all those bottles and tubes and cans, Katie. I'm having a new cleaning lady today and I don't want—"

"Mother! You're having a cleaning lady? What if she gets killed too?"

"Katie, don't be ridiculous!"

Jane said it with a conviction she didn't feel. Lightning doesn't strike twice in the same place, she'd been telling herself, but that didn't necessarily apply to murder. At least, she supposed it didn't. Still, she went back and gave Katie a hug that both pleased and embarrassed her. "Don't worry, kiddo."

As she headed out later with her first car pool, she noticed the red MG back in front of the Nowacks'. Now that Paul was back, VanDyne was probably questioning him. *Did Paul Nowack have enemies who might have had something to do with the murder?* Jane wondered. Who could guess? For, as much as she and Shelley saw of each other, Jane never felt she knew Paul at all. He traveled a great deal, and Jane had few opportunities to make her own assessment of him. As a neighbor, he was nice in a quiet way. But it wasn't any sort of shyness—more a sense of a powerful personality that was at rest. It had to be. How else would a Polish steelworker's boy turn into the man who owned a nationwide chain of Greek fast-food restaurants? That sort of thing didn't happen to wimpy men.

Questions started popping into her mind. Some pertinent, some idiotic. Why not Polish fast food, at least? Even if he were involved in something unsavory—which was highly unlikely—a disgruntled business enemy would hardly think killing his wife's cleaning lady would intimidate him.

Besides everything else, very few people had any idea where he lived. Shelley had said many times that he felt business was business and home was home. They even had an unlisted phone number, because he didn't want his franchisees being able to call him at home. In fact, his office staff didn't know how to find him; only his private secretary knew their home number. "The franchisees will call him in the middle of the night to ask how the dishwasher works otherwise," Shelley had said once when Jane asked about it.

That in itself was odd, now that she was thinking about it, in the light of a recent murder in the Nowack home. Was that really the reason for the unlisted number? Or was there a more sinister reason for keeping their number and address secret from the outside world? *That is ridiculous!* Jane told herself. Suspecting Paul of dark secrets was as insane as suspecting Shelley.

. . . suspecting Shelley? . . .

"No!" she said out loud.

"No what?" Mike asked.

She'd forgotten Mike and Katie were in the car. "Nothing. Just a crazy thought I had."

"You know what they say about people who talk to themselves," Katie said meaningfully.

"No, and I don't want to know," she said.

Jane dropped Katie off at the junior high and Mike and his group at the high school. Mike had the wisdom to refrain from asking to drive this morning, which she thought showed a nice sense of maturity. When she got back home, Todd was sitting on the front porch, playing with a neighborhood cat.

"Todd, I told you to stay inside with the house locked until Mrs. Wallenberg got here," Jane said. She must not have worded it strongly enough in her efforts to keep from frightening him with the implications.

"I know, but she called and said her car won't start and could you drive us today?"

"Oh, dear. All right. Hop in," Jane said, glancing at her watch. She'd wanted to be sure to be here when the cleaning lady arrived, but that was hardly reason to make the whole bunch of kids late for school.

Dorothy Wallenberg was in her driveway, pacing around on sturdy legs and slashing at grass blades with a tennis racket when Jane arrived. Obviously, this car problem was going to interfere with more than her car pool plans. "I'm so sorry, Jane."

"No problem, I was up and out anyway. Do you need help getting your car to the shop or anything?"

"No, they're supposed to be sending someone with a

tow truck pretty soon, and I haven't got anything going today that can't be cancelled. Stop back by and tell me what Shelley's found out."

"I can't, Dorothy. I've got Edith coming myself today. Maybe later on."

"You're having Edith? Why?"

"Well, I'm told she's terrific and I need somebody."

"I keep hearing how wonderful she is, Jane, but I had her for a month once and it was a waste of money. The woman just slouched around, pretending to work. 'A-lick-and-a-dab' cleaning, as my mother used to say. I complained to the Happy Helper people and they sent me somebody else."

"How odd. Robbie Jones says she's terrific, and so does Mary Ellen Revere. Even Joyce Greenway swears by her, and you know what a cleaning fanatic she is."

Dorothy laughed. "I went over once, and Joyce came to the door apologizing for taking so long. She'd been in the storeroom dusting the luggage, she told me. I thought she meant she was getting ready to go somewhere, so I said, 'Oh, why is that?' Do you know what she said? She said because it was Tuesday, of course."

Jane was still chuckling when she dropped Todd and his car pool off at the grade school. She detoured by way of the grocery store to make a quick foray for cleaning materials. She'd meant to take a careful inventory the day before, but had naturally forgotten about it in all the upset. Not knowing what she might be nearly out of, she dashed down the aisle, grabbing one of anything that might clean floors, tubs, sink stains, carpet spots, ovens, windows, even silver polish. The stuff cost a fortune. She consoled herself with the thought that it would all come in handy sooner or later.

She passed the Stapler's house. The red MG was parked in front. VanDyne must be questioning everyone. Her attention was soon diverted as she passed the Happy Helper van going the other way at the end of the street, and had a horrible shock as she pulled in her driveway. It was like yesterday, but a mirror image—her house instead of Shelley's. Standing at her kitchen door was Mrs. Thurgood!

Jane slammed on the brakes and the woman turned.

No, of course it wasn't the dead cleaning lady, but she was of a similar build with frizzy, blond hair. That and the blue uniform gave a scary impression.

"You must be Edith," Jane said, hoping the fact that she was carrying a huge, heavy sack would account for her breathlessness.

"That's right," Edith said, without offering to help. She merely stood back like company as Jane struggled to fit her key in the lock while balancing the cleaning materials. This didn't bode well, but then the woman's job didn't really start until she got inside. Jane knew her opinions of the moment were being influenced by Dorothy Wallenberg's claims. Still, it was odd that people had such widely different impressions of Edith.

While Jane showed her around and mentioned a few of the things she was particularly concerned about having done, Edith just sauntered along behind her, making the occasional affirmative noise. Jane couldn't figure out whether the woman took it all as a matter of course, or whether she simply wasn't interested in what Jane was saying. Neither of them referred to the events of the day before, even though it was obvious Edith must have known what had befallen her substitute. Jane kept feeling she ought to say something sympathetic, but didn't know what.

The tour was mercifully interrupted by the phone. Jane left Edith to strip the beds and ran downstairs to answer it. It was Uncle Jim.

"Honey, I just read the papers. That was right on your block, wasn't it? Are you all right?"

"You mean the murder? Yes, it was next door, at Shelley's, but I'm fine. Just kinda shaky."

"You want me to come stay with you until this is sorted out? I don't like to think about you and the kids there by yourselves."

"That's nice of you to offer, but you'd have an hour and a half drive each way to work."

"I wouldn't mind."

"Well, I would. No, I'm okay. Really. See you Sunday."

She had only a half hour before driving her blind kids, but she took the time for a quick shower and sprayed on a tiny, precious bit of the Giorgio perfume to which she'd treated herself for her birthday. These kids, having lost one sense, had developed the others to a high degree. It was a running joke with them to guess what sort of soap and shampoo she'd used, and they could often tell if she'd been to the store recently because of the scent of onions or cleaning materials or whatever she'd carted around in the station wagon.

As she flew through the kitchen, she found Edith leaning on the counter, gazing out the window and languidly sipping at a cup of coffee. There was no sign of her having done any cleaning at all.

Jane had a delightful morning with her kids. They identified the perfume right away, and knew about the cleaning materials. One of them also pointed out that there was a weak spot in the upholstery in the back seat, and the muffler didn't sound at all good.

The previous spring Jane had told the teacher that, come the new school year, she wanted to start learning how to help these kids in a more concrete way than simply acting as taxi driver. So, during class, she was blindfolded. "You can't pretend you're blind, Mrs. Jeffry," the teacher said. "You won't be really motivated unless you experience not seeing."

Jane acquired a few bruises trying to get through a maze of chairs using a cane, and discovered she had insensitive, if not downright numb, fingertips when she was introduced to braille. Still, as she drove home, she felt she'd gained valuable insight into what these children faced.

The experience gave her a lot to think about. Back in February, when Steve died, her great-aunt May had phoned to say, "My dear, I'm going to tell you the best advice I got when I was widowed and I want you to follow it. Do nothing for a year. Make no changes, no decisions that aren't necessary. Too many new widows dash into things they shouldn't before they've come to terms with their loss."

It was, she'd discovered, good advice, and she was glad she'd taken it, but now, little more than halfway through the first year, she was feeling impatient. She must *do* something. The children were growing up fast; in a few years they wouldn't need her so much. But she would still have whole days to fill. She needed to start planning how she was going to fill them.

It was probably too late now, but by the spring semester she was going to start some courses at the local junior college. She wanted to find out what else she might like and be good at besides mothering. Working with the blind children might be exactly that avenue.

When she got home, the kitchen was actually clean. Not spotless, by any means, but better than when she left. She had come in very quietly, not exactly admitting to herself that she wanted to sneak up on Edith, but doing so just the same. Dorothy's remarks about the cleaning lady just slouching around kept echoing in her mind. She wanted to know at what pace the woman worked when she was unsupervised. The vacuum cleaner was sitting in the living room and the magazines were straightened up. She ran her finger over the coffee table and sighed. No dusting had been done. There was no sign of Edith.

She went upstairs, hating herself for being so stealthy. No sign of her there, either, although the beds were made. She must be doing the family room in the base-ment. The last step creaked—it always did and Jane had forgotten—so she abandoned her sneaking. "Edith? Are you here?"

From the small adjoining office, Edith answered. "You're going to have a mildew problem down here if you don't get some circulation. Spiders too." She emerged, carrying a feather duster, and frowned sourly at Jane.

"I thought I told you I didn't want anything done in there." Jane was irritated. The office was off limits to everyone, even the kids. Steve had worked there, and she'd taken it over last winter for bill-paying and just plain hiding out. She considered it her own ward of a sort of personal mental health institute. It was the one place she could go and be absolutely alone when the pressure built up. She resented any intrusion. She was sure she had told Edith not to do the room, but Edith must not have been listening. Neither did she appear chagrined at the mistake.

"Those webs will get in the typewriter and make a mess of it," Edith said, clumping up the steps. It was clear that the discussion was over as far as she was concerned.

Suddenly Jane felt unaccountably depressed. She'd come home so buoyant, and now, because of a trivial irritation, she was deflated. These spells had come over her frequently last winter and spring, but over the summer, with the kids around all the time they had become less of a problem. Now that school had started and the regular routine was beginning, would she be subject to them again? Shelley had told her she should see a shrink, something about grief therapy, but she had found therapy of her own.

She closed the door, sat down in the butt-sprung chair, popped a tape of the *1812 Overture* into the tiny cassette player she kept in the top drawer, and leaned back with her feet on the desk top. She closed her eyes and let the music take her away. Within a few minutes, she was smiling and directing the orchestra.

Chapter Seven

Jane would have had a whole, precious hour of solitude if Shelley hadn't phoned. "Jane, you *are* going to that PTA meeting at the junior high this afternoon, aren't you?" she asked briskly.

"Are you crazy?"

"Good. I'm so glad. Early planning for the spring fund-raising carnival is so important."

"You *have* gone mad. You can't have forgotten the last one. The time I had to run the cotton candy machine and got that goo in my hair and vowed never to become involved again."

"I knew you'd feel that way. I'm looking forward to seeing you there. I'd give you a ride, but *Paul* is dropping me off."

"I see. Paul's there and you can't say what you mean."

"Wonderful. Yes, of course. See you then."

Jane gave some serious thought to the nature of friendship before dragging herself to the junior high. This seemed too high a price to pay. But, if Shelley was desperate enough to attend such a meeting, Jane's curiosity alone was roused to the point of enduring the setting to find out what was up.

She parked at the front of the big circle drive, the better to escape when the opportunity came. She had to sit quite still, getting her nerves under control, before she could enter the building. In Jane's opinion, junior high schools were possibly the worst idea educators had ever come up with. At the age children most needed to have older teens to look up to and younger children to set examples for, the system pulled them out and isolated them to flounder around without guidance. No, not without guidance; they had nearly as many couselors as teachers assigned to the school, but those supposedly trained adults hadn't a fraction of the influence the mere presence of exalted high school kids would have had.

Drawing a deep breath, Jane entered the school. Unfortunately, at that moment, the bell rang for the last class change and she found herself engulfed in a tide of children. A good third of the boys towered over her and half of them tripped over her. She was jostled unmercifully as she struggled to make her way to the art room, where the meeting was to be held. Some of the kids ran into her deliberately, some because they weren't paying attention, and a few because the poor things simply didn't know where all the parts of their rapidly developing bodies were at any given moment. Twice, as she clawed her way forward, a timid voice greeted her by name. She couldn't discern the source either time.

She thought she glimpsed Katie, but made no attempt to get her attention. That would have been asking for a snub. She knew that junior high schoolers always tried to maintain the fiction that they had no parents. They might, if pressed, grudgingly admit to a father for the sake of filling out forms, but not to a mother. And never in public.

She all but fell into the art room when she finally reached it. There were about twenty women present, most of them more or less familiar. Grade-school PTAs consisted of a beleaguered cross section of parents. By junior high, however, only the truly devoted club women were involved. These were the folks they should have called on to bail out Chrysler; they'd have staged international bake sales to boggle the mind. Small knots of conversation were breaking up, and the women were moving (with obscene eagerness, it seemed to Jane) toward desks so the meeting could commence.

"It positively reeks of hormones in this building," one of them was muttering to her friend.

"It isn't all hormones. It's dirty gym socks and chalk dust too. And cheap perfume," the friend replied.

Before Jane could contribute her opinion, Shelley appeared and dragged her to the back of the room, where she'd staked out two desks for them. "Thank God!" Jane exclaimed. "I thought you'd gotten me here and not shown up yourself. What is it?"

"Remember when Paul's mother died a year ago?" Shelley was talking fast, anxious to convey as much as possible before the group was called to order.

"Huh? Yes, but what on earth—?"

"Well, she left him—not me, mind you, but him—a strand of pearls that belonged to her mother. They're missing."

"Forgive me, but what in the world are you talking about? A strand of *real* pearls? But I thought—"

"—that Paul's people were dirt poor. Right. I don't know if the pearls are genuine or not. See, his mother emigrated from Poland just after World War I with her parents. The pearls were supposed to have been given to her folks during the war by some Russian soldier they helped escape a firing squad or some such thing. They were probably trash, but they might have been the result of some high-class looting. For all I know he might have ripped them off Anastasia's neck."

"You never told me."

"I never took the story seriously. They looked pretty ratty to me. Kinda discolored and lumpy. It crossed my mind that they were just tightly rolled dough lumps with a little varnish. Anyhow, Paul thought they were *the* family treasure, and said he was going to take them to New York sometime and have them appraised and cleaned and re-strung. In the meantime, he told me to put them in the safe-deposit box."

"Ladies! let me have your attention . . ." a woman at the front of the room said, clapping her hands in a very school-teacherish way. She was an angular, hard-featured woman with a belligerent manner. The kid who tried to jostle her in the halls probably came away with serious bruises.

Jane lowered her voice. "Am I to assume you didn't bother to lock them up?"

"Exactly. I just forgot. They were in an envelope in the drawer with my bras and slips and now they're gone."

"Now, as you know, the carnival is our primary source of revenue for the purchase of an annual gift. Ladies? In the back! Could I please have your attention?"

Jane and Shelley pretended interest for a few moments, and when the speaker had lost interest in policing them, Jane whispered out of the side of her mouth, "Why is this a secret? Have you told VanDyne?"

"No. I don't want Paul to know."

"But, Shelley, the police have to know. It surely has a bearing on the motive for the murder."

"Maybe . . ."

"How many of you ladies have worked the annual carnival before?" the speaker was asking.

Jane obediently put her arm up and went on whispering to Shelley. "So why are you telling me this before you've told them?"

"I just can't have Paul knowing. It might be a mistake. I mean, maybe I did put them in the box at the bank and just forgot."

"You know better! Have you ever had amnesia before?"

"I can't remember," Shelley said, smiling feebly.

"I'm serious. You have to tell VanDyne, no matter how upset Paul might get. What's the worst he can do?"

"He won't *do* anything except be terribly hurt that I was so neglectful of something that meant so much to his whole family. Jane, I think you should—"

"Thank you, Mrs. Jeffry. I knew we could count on you."

"—put your arm down."

"Count on me?" Jane asked, fearing the worst.

"I think you just volunteered to run the cotton candy machine again."

"Shit!"

After this, in self-defense, she gave her full attention to the meeting in progress. It broke up moments before the final bell, and she and Shelley fled. No self-respecting adult would set themselves up for being in the building at the final bell on a Friday afternoon. "Jane, I want you to talk to the police for me," Shelley said, once they were breathing fresh, free air again.

"Shelley, I can't do that. For one thing, VanDyne already thinks I'm half-crazy and wouldn't believe me. He'd run straight to Paul to confirm the story and get a description of the pearls—or bread pellets or whatever they are."

"Then they just aren't going to know."

"The police *have* to know. It's important to their investigation."

"I'm not so sure. Jane, hasn't it struck you as odd? The whole thing? I mean, nobody knew I even had the damned things except Paul's family, and none of them live anywhere near. So why would some random thief come in my house, ignore the silver, the home computer, the stereo, the other jewelry—all that stuff they usually steal—and go straight to my underwear drawer to steal a string of highly questionable pearls?"

"Of course it's odd. But what do you think it means?"

"I have no idea."

Further discussion was cut short by the clanging of the final bell. Within seconds they were buffeted by kids escaping the building. "There's Paul, parked up the street. I've got to go."

"But we haven't settled anything." Jane raised her voice over the sounds of chaos around her.

"No, but I'll figure out what to do. Don't worry," Shelley said. "See you later."

Jane went back to the relative safety of her car to wait for Katie to emerge from school. She lit a cigarette and sat staring sightlessly at the crowd of kids swarming past. The whole situation was very strange. Why *would* someone ignore all the other obviously valuable things in Shelley's home and go straight to the possibly fake string of pearls? She had said Paul's family all lived somewhere else, but suppose one of them had slipped into town and taken the necklace? Still, even if that were true, how would anybody know where she kept them? Shelley certainly hadn't sat around after the funeral and said to Paul's family that she thought she'd just take the pearls home and put them in with her slips and bras.

The house hadn't shown any overt signs of ransacking. Even a subtle search would have been apparent to Shelley, considering the kind of meticulous housekeeper she was. No, it would seem that somebody knew exactly where to look. And nobody but Shelley herself knew where they were. Even Paul thought they were safely in the bank.

A nasty little thought was flitting around the back of her mind. If Shelley was the only one who knew where they were, could she be faking a theft? Jane shook her head as if to physically dispel the notion. Why in the world would Shelley do that, and what kind of friend would suspect her?

"What were you doing in the school?" Katie asked, flinging the door open and startling Jane.

"Wasting time. Inadvertently volunteering to work at the carnival," Jane replied sourly.

"Oh, Mother! Do you have to come?"

No, Jane thought, *with any luck I'll die before then*. Of course, that woman in charge would probably just prop her up behind the cotton candy booth and expect her to do her job anyway.

Chapter Eight

Shelley phoned as Jane was running in the door. She explained that Paul didn't want her to be frightened by staying in the house until the killer was found. They were going to a hotel ten miles away.

"I don't like hotels, and I don't mind in the least staying in the house as long as he's home, so I'll talk him out of this tomorrow, but . . . dinner out and a night alone will be nice," she added in a husky whisper. "I've got a beautiful nightgown that Suzie talked me into buying months ago—"

"Have you told him?"

"No."

"Or the police?"

"Detective VanDyne called, but they don't seem to know anything. Either they're blundering around in the dark or they're just not telling us about their leads. Gotta go! Paul's rattling the car keys. I'll be back tomorrow afternoon. Talk to you then."

As Jane was speaking, Edith was putting on her sweater and changing from the carpet slippers she wore to work in to more attractive shoes. The light blue van was already parked at the curb. Jane hadn't had a chance to really look over the house, but planned to do so before the kids could start messing it up again. She handed Edith a five-dollar bill. The Happy Helper people would bill her for Edith's services by mail, but it was customary to give an extra tip.

Before she could escape to a quiet place to think over all Shelley had said, Katie reminded her that they hadn't gotten their allowances the day before, due to the upheaval next door.

"But I have to have my money today. Jenny and I are going shopping tonight."

"With whom?"

"Oh, Mother!"

"Don't 'oh, Mother' me. You know I don't approve of teenagers aimlessly cruising the mall."

"Mother, that's so old-fashioned. Nobody else's mother—"

"You know what I'm going to say to that, no matter where the sentence is going, don't you?"

"I know. That you don't care what anybody else's mother does," she said in a singsong imitation of Jane's refrain. "Anyway, Jenny's mom is going with us. She's getting some fabric, and Jenny is going to buy some false fingernails."

In other words, the whole dispute was theoretical, Jane thought. Sort of like testing a locked door at intervals just in case it might be unlocked. She remembered doing the same thing herself. She also remembered fake fingernails. She had put some on just before going to bed once when she was about that age and woke up with them all stuck in her hair. No point in telling Katie that. She'd find out for herself. Every generation has to reinvent the wheel.

Jane went back down to the basement office. The kids weren't the only ones who needed money. The five she had given Edith had been the last money in her billfold. Normally, she got their allowances and cash for groceries every Thursday morning, but this hadn't exactly been a normal week. She had a carry-around checkbook for emergency expenses, but regular bills and this weekly cash withdrawal were always written from the money market checkbook she kept locked in the desk. Steve had started the system, and she'd stuck with it out of habit.

She pulled open the middle drawer and reached under it for the little magnetic box stuck on the underside. Again, a policy of Steve's she'd stayed with for no other reason than the fact that they'd always done it that way.

From the box, she removed the key to the deep bottom right drawer. But the key wouldn't go in. That was odd.

She leaned over to see what the problem was. The little vertical slot was horizontal. The drawer was already unlocked. She must have failed to lock it last Friday. No, that wasn't right. She remembered how annoyed she'd been because she'd broken her best fingernail when she had flipped the key back up last week. Had she opened it since then? She thought not; except for that hour earlier in the afternoon, she hadn't even been in the office.

Her suspicions growing, Jane studied the drawer contents before lifting out the checkbook. All her really valuable papers were in the safe-deposit box at the bank— the abstract on the house, copies of income tax forms, birth certificates, wills. This drawer was a second-string-valuables storage area—the kids' report cards, some family pictures, receipts for major purchases, warranties on the appliances, some foreign money she'd collected in her childhood, an envelope with the kids' baby teeth, and, of course, the money market checkbook.

It was a hodgepodge drawer without any particular system, but she only tidied it up about once a year, so she had a sort of petrified vision of what it should all look like. And it didn't look right. She couldn't have said what was out of order, as there was no order, but she had a strong sense that it had been rearranged.

Bending down, she studied the lock. There was a fresh-looking scratch at the side of the keyhole. The key itself had a rounded end, so she couldn't have made it herself. She took out the checkbook. Nothing was missing. Rummaging in the drawer again, she found everything that should have been there. She wrote the check she needed and returned everything to the drawer, then locked it carefully and put the key back in the little magnetic box.

"If I were going to pick a lock . . ." she said to herself as she looked through the things in the top middle drawer. It didn't take long to find the perfect tool (or so she assumed, having had little experience with lock-picking since her sister had given up keeping a locked diary twenty-five years ago); a miniature screwdriver in a glasses-repair kit. She unscrewed the top of the kit and shook the contents out in her hand. Tiny screws and a little magnifying glass tumbled out, but no screwdriver. That she was sure she had not lost. Her favorite sunglasses kept losing screws, and she guarded the little kit as if it were made of gold.

She closed the drawer and sat back in the comfortable old chair. The only person who'd been in the room, besides herself, was Edith. She tried to recall whether there had been any hint of guilt in Edith's manner when she caught her in the room. Not guilt, but a bit of defensiveness, maybe, in that critical remark about mildew and spiders. Jane closed her eyes and tried to recall whether she'd heard the drawer close. No, but then it was a wooden drawer on runners and it closed silently, unless you shoved it hard enough to slam.

There was also the fact that Jane was certain she'd specifically told Edith not to go in the office. She'd assumed Edith just hadn't paid attention—but if you were looking for something valuable, wouldn't you look in the one room you were told not to go in? Not having criminal inclinations much beyond snooping in sisters' diaries, Jane was straining with the effort to imagine what a criminal would think.

But was Edith a criminal? Nothing valuable was missing. If she didn't steal anything, what was she doing? Probably getting ready to steal something when Jane interrupted. Or possibly she just didn't find Jane's treasures worth stealing. Jane smiled wryly. That was vaguely insulting, in a funny way.

Still, if she was a thief...

Closing up the office, Jane did a quick survey of the house. Edith had carried only a small purse, so she couldn't have taken anything big. The little silver matchbox was in the living room; it had even been polished, though the cleaning woman had left some polishing gunk in the cracks. The antique coloisonné cigarette jar was in place, as were all the coins in Steve's framed collection in the hallway. The silver was safely locked in its drawer in the china cabinet. Todd's piggy bank was intact and obviously full. Her own jewelry was all in the box on her dressing table. . . .

She spent half an hour doing a mental inventory before deciding that nothing was gone. She thought about it all the way to the bank and back, and then, sitting down at the kitchen table with a fresh cup of coffee, Jane brooded. The woman had had hours alone in the house while Jane was with the blind kids. She could have taken any number of things, if she'd wanted. So why wasn't anything gone? Feeling that she might have misjudged, Jane still was at a loss to explain the unlocked desk drawer. There was no question in her mind that the lock had been picked and the contents pawed through.

So what would explain it? Think logically, she told herself. Like yesterday, when she and Shelley were discussing reasons for murder. And was there any connection between the missing pearls and the missing screwdriver? How could there be? Rummaging in her purse for the scrap of paper with Shelley's hotel number on it, she dialed.

"Shelley, are you doing anything?"

"My nails. Paul is taking me downtown for dinner. He's in the other room in the suite right now making some business calls."

The other room of the suite . . . Jane didn't comment on how the Nowacks spent a night away from home. The last time she and Steve had spent a night alone together it had been in a Holiday Inn room, next to the elevator shaft.

"Shelley, I understand you can't talk about the pearls, but I want to discuss something odd with you. Just to sort out my own thoughts." She explained about the unlocked desk drawer and her suspicions. Throughout, Shelley made no comment. There was only the occasional *whhh* as she blew on her nails.

"You think Edith did it, then?" Shelley asked when Jane was through with her recital.

"I think so, yes. But for some reason, I don't want to believe it—or there's something wrong with the assumption. I just want to eliminate all the other possibilities."

"Hmmm, I guess you have to consider that someone else might have gone through the desk drawer."

"But who? The kids?"

"Not very likely suspects, I agree," Shelley said.

"Mike's too moral and upright. I'd never dream of accusing him of that to his face—it isn't what teenagers want to be called—but it's true. He's always the one who makes me go back and fess up when I accidentally get too much change from a clerk."

"There speaks a proud mother," Shelley said with a laugh.

"No, it's not that I have any illusions about his faults; he has plenty, including his cavalier attitude toward my mental health and well-being when in a car. But he utterly lacks any sneakiness. If he wanted to look in the drawer, he'd have just asked for the key—and I'd have given it to him, and he knows it."

"One down and two to go. Eliminate Katie. *Whhh*—" Shelley said, blowing on another nail.

"Katie? Katie can be sneaky. It goes with the age and gender."

"Doesn't it just!"

"I think the urge to experiment with the truth to see just how far it can be bent is part of the growing-up process. But Katie wouldn't have broken into the drawer— she's already stripped me of all my valuables. If she thought there was anything she might want in there, she'd have just nagged until I gave it to her. That's how she got the little pearl pinkie ring away from me."

"The one she lost in the swimming pool?"

"That's the one."

"All right, what about Todd? *Whhh*—"

"He's very good at mechanical things, and sheer curiosity might have made him pick the lock just to see what was in there, except he was the one who helped me last time I cleaned out the drawer. Back in March, when he had the chicken pox. He was driving me crazy, fetching things for him, so I made him help. He knows everything that's in it, and found most of it real boring. All he liked was some Mexican coins I had in there, and I gave them to him. So he had no reason to get into it."

"What about you? Couldn't you have gone through it and just forgotten about it?"

No, Jane thought. A year or two ago it might have been possible. When the kids were smaller and she was more harried and hadn't adjusted to the maternal necessities of balancing five schedules in her head—then, it might have been possible. But since last winter, this quiet little office had become a special haven, and she simply didn't allow the rush of daily life to interfere. It was a little like self-hypnosis; she'd conditioned herself to the state that the very act of stepping in the door served to make her think calmly. She could picture herself doing any sort of loony, scatterbrained thing almost anywhere but here.

"I'm certain I didn't leave it unlocked or mess up the drawer, and even if I had, why is the eyeglasses screwdriver missing?"

"*Whhh*—So, if it wasn't one of you—and temporarily assuming it wasn't the obvious Edith, just for fairness—who else could it have been? Who else came in the house? What about the kids' friends? You haven't had that Stringer child in, have you?"

"Lord, no! Didn't they put him away for the Brinks robbery in fifth grade?"

"No, I think they may have moved to Cleveland."

"Same thing. There are armies of kids through here all the time, but very few since last week because of school starting. Besides, they're in the kitchen pillaging the refrigerator or in the living room with the video games when they visit. None of the kids' friends would be caught dead in the basement family room."

"Not wishing to speak ill of the dead—Jane, now that Steve's gone, why don't you give up calling that a 'family room' and just refer to it as the dank, hideous cave it is?"

"Steve worked so hard on it—"

"Yes, and if he'd been a carpenter or electrician—or better yet, a foundation specialist—instead of a pharmacist, it might have turned out nicely. But that's beside the point. You feel certain it wasn't a kid who got into the desk drawer?"

"Shelley, it seemed too—I don't know how to put it—too cunning and careful to be the act of a kid. Someone looked for a good tool without any obvious rummaging in the center drawer. And they didn't root around violently in the other drawer either. The disturbance was subtle; I probably wouldn't have noticed if I hadn't been suspicious to begin with because the lock was wrong. It's like with your pearls. Somebody seemed to know exactly where to go without messing anything else up."

"Bad subject."

"I know you can't talk about it at your end. I was just mentioning it."

Shelley went on as if jewelry had never been mentioned. "Well, I think you've pretty well cleared all the other possible suspects, unless you've had any service people in lately. Had anything repaired in the basement?"

"Nobody."

"Then I think you're stuck with assuming it was Edith."

"But why? She didn't steal anything."

"Maybe she was just checking out what there was to steal later on, when you're used to her being around."

"I don't know—I'm reluctant to believe badly of her. But I think I'm going to fire her anyway, because she depresses the hell out of me."

"Don't worry, Jane. There are plenty of people who will be delighted to sign up for her. Her customers speak so highly of her."

"Not everybody." Jane repeated Dorothy Wallenberg's remarks.

"That's funny. Dorothy's not real fussy. I dropped an earring between her sofa cushions at a party once, and when I reached down, I found an Easter egg. It was a Christmas party. I wouldn't think she'd demand perfection. Do you know what? I think we've both gone a little nutty because of the murder. A week ago we'd have never had a conversation this long over something so trivial."

"Who are you trying to kid? We once spent a whole hour analyzing Mary Ellen Revere's makeup. Remember?"

Shelley laughed. "Paul's through with his calls. Gotta go—*whhh*—I'll think of you over my shrimp salad and raspberry torte."

"What kind of thing is that to say to a friend who's planning hot dogs and baked beans for dinner?"

When she'd hung up, Jane went to the window and

looked out at Shelley's house. The red MG was there again. Poor Detective VanDyne—he was probabaly bored and hungry. Maybe she could make a decent dinner and invite him over. She glanced in the refrigerator. There were possibilities there. But as she closed the door, she caught sight of her reflection in the microwave door.

"Katie!" she called up the stairs. "Buy me some of those fingernails while you're out, would you? And some mascara and blusher . . ."

Chapter Nine

Jane had planned to spend a quiet evening with the kids, but it didn't work out that way. Todd got an invitation to spend the night with Elliot Wallenberg, an invitation he was dying to accept because of Elliot's new toys from his birthday earlier in the week. Katie was asked to sleep over with Jenny after their shopping trip. Jenny, a chunky girl who ate like part of a starving nation, had spent the night with the Jeffrys a half dozen times over the summer, and Jane felt it would help even the score.

Mike's marching band was playing at the first football game of the season. Both the musicians and the athletes had been practicing since weeks before school started and were chomping at the bit. He was going out for pizza afterwards with a friend whose parents had rashly bought him a car for his birthday. Mike was making noises as if he was expecting the same bounty to befall him. Jane had tried to make him understand that she could hardly afford to keep her station wagon running now that he was on the insurance. Another vehicle wasn't possible. Of course, there was always the possibility that Thelma would step into the breach, checkbook in hand. The thought made Jane mad, but she could never figure out quite why.

Their departure left Jane alone and at the mercy of the phone. Everyone seemed to feel it was tacky to call Shelley and ask for the gruesome details of the murder. A few had no such delicate feelings, but simply couldn't reach her. They all called Jane. By ten o'clock her mouth felt cottony from talking, and her brain was stewed from

70

repeating the few things she did know over and over. There was really so little to say, so little known.

Each caller seemed to have a theory of her own. The vagrant maniac was a popular theme, possibly because that meant they were safe—how many vagrant maniacs are there, after all? And a vagrant maniac doesn't hang around the neighborhood. He moves on to Dubuque, or Fargo.

A woman from the next block who was active in the John Birch Society was certain it was a Communist plot. Her theory had something to do with oppressed workers, though Jane refrained from pointing out that accusing the 'commies' of killing one of the oppressed hardly made sense.

Another neighbor, having read in the paper that the victim had previously lived in Montana, figured it all had to do with a survivalist group from which Ramona Thurgood had very likely escaped with some kind of secret information.

"But she had a newspaper route and taught Sunday school," Jane protested to this one. "Survivalists don't do things like that."

"Jane, dear, you're too, too naïve. They have people in every walk of life. That's what's so insidious. Why, all you have to do is watch the children's cartoons to see that they've infiltrated the toy industry. The cartoons themselves are rife with violence, and then the commercials are for toy soldiers and tanks. Who do you suppose provided the money to make "Rambo"? They're poisoning the minds of a whole generation. It's pitiful. I suspect we may someday regard this poor woman, who died trying to warn us of their plans, as a genuine heroine."

Jane hung up, shaking her head in wonder.

The last call was Joyce Greenway. "I'm so worried about you and the children staying in the house alone."

"We're not alone. There is a whole mob of us."

"I mean without a man to protect you. Won't you please come stay with us until this is over?"

I'm sick to death of Joyce's well-meant sympathy, Jane thought, but managed to put a smile in her voice. "That's really nice of you, Joyce. But we're really just fine."

Finally, at ten, the phone stopped ringing and Jane

was able to settle in to watching an old Katharine Hepburn movie, until Mike got home and bored her with a detailed account of the school football game. She slept soundly that night—no dreams of murder, no dreams at all.

Jane tried to sneak out in the morning to pick Katie and Todd up, but at the first muted jingle of car keys, Mike appeared. "I'll drive!" he said blearily.

"I thought you were still asleep. In fact, I still think you are." She gave him a light punch on the arm and he collapsed against the counter.

"Just give me a sec, Mom. I'll be ready."

The pickups were completed without incident. Todd gave an enthusiastic but exceedingly tedious rundown of Elliot's new acquisitions, with strong suggestions as to which of the same he needed for Christmas. Jane listened patiently, knowing he'd be tired of them by then and have a new list. Then, by February, he'd start compiling yet another. Mike graciously made no critical older-brother comments about the length or content of Todd's accounting.

Katie's fingernails were hideous, and she was positively thrilled with them. "I think they make my hands look so thin—don't you, Mom?"

Jane thought they looked more like a medical condition than a beauty aid, but took note of the "Mom" instead of "Mother" and was effusive in her compliments. Again Mike said nothing. He made a perfectly repulsive noise through his nose, but didn't actually speak.

By the time they pulled in the drive, Jane was thoroughly mellowed by how nice and family-ish they were being. They had a late-morning snack that was a cross between breakfast and lunch, then Jane took Todd to his last baseball game of the season.

"You don't need to stay, Mom," he offered.

"I always stay. Aren't you pitching?"

"Only the first inning. The coach said since we don't have any chance of the championship, he's gonna let everybody pitch."

"Well, I'll probably stay anyway."

"You don't need to," he insisted.

The problem was suddenly clear. They were having a big picnic after the game, and Todd didn't want his freedom to enjoy himself hampered by her presence. Since it was already arranged that another mother would bring the car pool home, he'd counted on attending as a "bachelor," so to speak.

"Okay, I'll just watch your inning."

He smiled. "Thanks, Mom-Old-Thing."

When they reached the field, he and the three boys they'd picked up fled and Jane hung back, checking out who was there. There were mothers one never got near at these games, women who made George Steinbrenner look like Heidi. Happily, she spotted Suzie Williams and picked her way up the bleachers to join her.

Suzie was one of her favorite people. She was a big divorcée who would have been called "handsome" in an earlier age. She had long, platinum-blond hair and a gorgeous complexion. Her cheeks were always naturally pink, and her eyes were glacial-blue. She looked like an earthy Swedish queen who'd been hitting the smorgasbord a little too heavily.

She saw Jane coming and put down the blood-and-guts paperback novel she'd been reading. "Good God, it's Jane Jeffry, font of murderous gossip. I imagine you're being driven mad by nosy neighbors callously invading your privacy and peace of mind? Most people are so insensitive."

"What do you want to know?"

"Everything! Every bloody detail!"

Jane gave her account by rote. She'd told it so many times it hardly seemed real anymore. The one thing she didn't mention was the missing pearls. That was, unfortunately, Shelley's secret, and Jane felt bound to honor it, even if she disapproved.

"Shelley might have talked to the police again by now and found out something more, but she wasn't home when I came out. She and Paul are staying at a hotel."

"Hiding from the killer?"

"No, I think they're having an orgy."

"If I could get my hands on Paul Nowack, I'd have an

orgy too. Ever seen him in swimming trunks? Oh, to die for—! Anyhow, who do you think killed her?"

"I haven't any idea."

"Too bad it wasn't the regular one that got knocked off. Edith, isn't that her name?"

"Why? What's the matter with Edith?"

"I don't know. I just didn't like her. I just had her once, and by the end of a day having her mooch around looking like she had a cob up her ass, I wanted to bang my head on the wall—or hers. Depressing bitch. Kept giving me these searching looks, like she was waiting for me to say something to take offense at. I probably obliged. I generally do."

"That's weird, Suzie. People have such different opinions of her. Dorothy Wallenberg didn't like her because she didn't clean very well—"

"Dorothy said that? The woman who had the patio party and didn't notice there was dog shit under the grill?"

"—and Robbie Jones thinks she's wonderful."

"Jesus God. You could eat out of Robbie's toilets! I had a salad there once that tasted sorta funny, and after a while I realized it was soap. When she washes lettuce, she *really* washes lettuce. And this cleaning woman meets *her* standards? Have you ever had her clean for you? Edith, I mean?"

"Yesterday. I felt like you did. She got me down. What's more—"

She was interrupted by a cheer from the parents around them as the two teams of little boys ran onto the field. "Cute little bastards, aren't they?" Suzie said affectionately.

After the requisite amount of fumbling around, the game got under way. Todd's team, which Suzie's son Bob was on as well, was in red and white, and were as crisp and noisy as firecrackers as they went to bat. There were a great many balls called and walks made and steals attempted, but at the end of the inning, only one run scored. Jane stayed on, thoroughly enjoying Suzie's vulgar commentary on the game, the parents, and life in general.

At the bottom half of the third inning, one kid on the other team made a long, high drive. The entire outfield ran for it, all looking up. A collision was inevitable. Three of them crashed together behind second base. The parents fell momentarily silent as the heap of children was sorted out. One of them was led from the field, limping ostentatiously.

"That's my Bob, the klutz," Suzie said, hoisting herself up and getting ready to go comfort him. She'd made it down three rows, stepping on purses and fingers with judicious abandon, when she stopped, shaded her eyes, and turned around and came back up. She sat down. "Wasn't Bob at all. It's that Jonnell kid. They all look alike in those uniforms."

The game resumed and so did Suzie. "We had the Jonnell family to a barbecue one night last summer, and I swear, the kid has the foulest mouth I've ever heard. And his mother! I saw her come within a hair of punching out the coach when he put the kid on the bench for it. Some people—Jane? Earth calling Jane? Are you there?"

Jane turned to her, eyes wide. "Could that be it? The uniforms?"

"What the hell are you talking about?"

Grabbing her arm, Jane leaned forward. "You said it was a shame it wasn't Edith killed instead of the other woman."

"I didn't really mean—"

"Shut up, Suzie. Listen. Nobody had any reason to kill the other woman, but there might be a reason to kill Edith. I don't know what, but suppose there was."

"Okay, what if there was?"

"Edith was supposed to be at Shelley's, and a woman in a Happy Helper uniform gets out of a Happy Helper van at the right house. They even looked alike, in a superficial way. Matter of fact, when Edith turned up at my house yesterday, it gave me a scare. I thought she was the other woman from a distance. They were both middle-sized, kinda hippy—"

"So who isn't?"

"—and they both had frizzy blond hair."

"So why didn't the killer notice they weren't the same person when he got up close?"

That stopped Jane for a minute. She leaned back,

thinking. "Because—because he must have come up behind her. Don't you usually vacuum with your back to the
doorway?"

"I never thought about it, but yes. I start with the
corners and back myself out."

"So the cleaning woman would have been working
with her back to the door, with the noise of the vacuum
cleaner covering any sound an attacker might have made.
He just had to pick up a loose loop of the cord, throw it
over her head and—twist," she finished with a shiver. The
memory of the dead Ramona Thurgood assaulted her, turning the mental exercise back into the real and very terrible
event it was.

"He might not have ever seen her face," Suzie agreed.
"You know, I think you may have something there, but you
still have one problem: why would anyone kill Edith,
assuming she *was* the intended victim? She's a distasteful
sort, but if we went around killing people for that, it
would be a pretty sparsely populated planet." She glanced
around her and added, "I can think of a few who could be
the first to go."

"I don't know—but I'm going to call that detective
and tell him my idea. He gave me a number when he
questioned me. In case I remembered anybody else who'd
come to Shelley's that day."

"This detective—is he good-looking?"

"Oh, I don't know—"

"Bullshit. That means he is. Why don't you go see
him instead of calling? You could take a divorced friend
along for moral support."

"I want him to pay attention to what I'm saying, not
to the gorgeous blonde drooling down his shirt front."

"Cruel, cruel."

Impatient to call the detective, Jane stopped at a pay
phone a block from the ball field. "Detective VanDyne,
this is Jane Jeffry, Shelley Nowack's next-door neighbor."

"I know who you are, Mrs. Jeffry."

Jane didn't preen, but she smiled. "I've figured out

the murder. Well, I haven't exactly figured out who did it, but—"

"That's the end result we like."

Jane bristled at this, but went on. "It had to do with uniforms. You see, one of the boys at the baseball game got hurt, and my friend Suzie thought it was her son because they all look alike in the uniforms, and that got me thinking—"

"—that the regular cleaning lady was the intended victim?"

"Oh." Jane was crushed. "You'd thought of that?"

"It's a natural thing to wonder when there doesn't appear to be any motive. It doesn't appear to be the case, but I'd be interested in hearing what supporting evidence you have for your assumption."

"Supporting evidence—? Oh, I see. Well, they looked alike. Not close up, but from the back, and when you vacuum, you usually have your back to the door."

"How interesting. Hmmm. I didn't know, of course, that the two women were similar, and that vacuuming thing is interesting. Only a housewife would think of it."

Jane had been considering telling him about Shelley's pearls. After all, Shelley had, at one point, asked her to do so. But his tone changed her mind. She considered just calling him a condescending bastard and hanging up; Suzie would have recommended it, she was sure. But she rejected that course as well. VanDyne wasn't going to find out anything more from her, but she might want to learn something from him.

"Well, thanks for listening," she said with venomous sweetness. "If there's ever anything else you want to know about housework, I'm your woman. Just call—I'll be in the kitchen trying to decide which paper towel is more absorbent."

"Say, you're not mad, are you?"

Furious, insulted, pissed as hell—

"No, I'm not mad, Detective VanDyne. Good-bye."

She really should have turned Suzie loose on him.

Chapter Ten

On three out of every four Sundays they all went to church. On the fourth the kids went, and Jane stayed home to get ready for dinner. She didn't usually need the time, but the occasional quiet Sunday morning alone was a blessing itself. This monthly family dinner had been another tradition Steve had started and she had continued—with a few alterations and under considerable pressure from her mother-in-law Thelma.

It was by no means the only hold she still had on Jane, but she used it to the hilt, as if Jane and the kids might escape her iron circle of influence if she didn't show up monthly to tighten up the "ties that bind."

These family dinners would have been unbearable if Thelma hadn't been diluted by the other guests. Steve's brother Ted and his wife Dixie Lee usually came along too. Ted was a quiet, pleasant man; not a thrilling conversationalist by any means, but amiable, and a neutralizing influence on his mother's antics. His wife Dixie Lee was an Oklahoma girl, hardly into her twenties, with a sweet disposition and an accent like warm molasses. To Jane's delight, Thelma disapproved of her even more heartily than she disapproved of Jane.

"She'd expected Ted to stay home with her forever," Jane had explained to Shelley two years ago when Ted fell for Dixie Lee. She had been hired to demonstrate a new line of beauty products in the family's main drug store, and Ted was instantly smitten. "Steve had escaped from Thelma's clutches when I—a scarlet woman if there ever was one—snared him. But *this* girl! Half Ted's age and too nice—or too dumb—to even notice Thelma's digs? It's too much for Thelma. She's about to go berserk."

After all this time, Thelma was still fuming and casting barbed remarks at Dixie Lee, and Dixie Lee was still blissfully unaware of them. Ted shared her attitude. If he had any idea of what his mother felt, he didn't let on. Nor did he seem the slightest bit influenced by her unceasing, attempts to denigrate his wife.

After Steve died, Jane had added a guest to the dinner roster: her honorary Uncle Jim, her father's life-long best friend. An ex-Army officer, he'd finished his twenty years and gone to work for the Chicago police department. Assigned to the most lawless part of the inner city, he was the happiest he'd ever been. Life among the pimps and pushers suited him right down to the ground.

"All I ever did in the Army was push papers around and go to drills for events that never happened," he explained. "In this job things are always happening, and from time to time I actually manage to do something worthwhile."

Thelma hated his intrusion into the family circle with a fervor that sometimes approached frenzy. The first time Jim had joined them, last February, she'd attacked Jane for inviting him.

"After all, my dear, he associates with such unacceptable people. One would hardly think he was a good influence on the children."

"He's associated with my parents for forty years!" Jane shot back. "I don't have them near me, but I *must* have him."

"But Jane, dear, we're your family now."

"Thelma, you make it sound like I'm a Middle-Eastern camel trader's daughter who's left her tribe for her husband's."

"Rather a vulgar analogy, don't you think?"

"What's vulgar? The Middle-East? Camels? Tribes?"

"Dear, you're just upset. We all understand. Steve's demise has been a devastating blow to all of us. I fear my own health has been permanently damaged by the distress. Now, let's don't talk about this anymore."

That was as close as she ever came to admitting she'd

lost a round. She hadn't given up her campaign to have sole ownership of Jane and the kids, but she didn't bring it up directly after that. Every month she sat across the table from Uncle Jim and glared her disapproval. He, bless his heart, found it amusing, and would occasionally wink at her just to see her blush with fury. Jane hoped he'd leave off this month, however. The day was just too nice for conflict.

When the kids got back from church, Jane was sitting on the patio, hypnotically scratching Willard's ears and quietly enjoying the smell of newly cut grass from the several lawns nearby. It would probably be the last Sunday for it. By next month, people would have stopped mowing for the winter, and there would begin to be the smell of burning leaves in the air. She'd observed that no amount of modern suburban restrictions seemed able to stop people from indulging in the primitive need to stand around a big outdoor fire on the first cool days.

Then, next spring, there would be the odors of fertilizer, and weed killer, and good brown earth returning from the winter sleep. Jane had always liked that best, but had missed it last spring. She'd still been grieving too deeply to take much notice of anything outside herself and the immediate concerns of getting from day to day without letting the kids know how upset she was. Next spring, however, she'd make up for it. Maybe a nice garden— Steve had never approved of gardens. He was a lawn man, taking inordinate pride in an unbroken spread of lush green.

The one thing Steve had hated about the house was the field behind it. The developers had apparently intended one more street between Jane's and the main drag, but had run out of money—or enthusiasm—before the last street was completed. The field had remained a field, much to the delight of Max and Meow, who spent all their free time out hunting. Steve, however, had despised the weeds that grew there and were perpetually trying to invade his precious lawn.

Jane got up and strolled around the yard, considering.

Gardens had always appealed to her need for permanence. A garden meant you were going to stay someplace. You planted leathery little brown bulbs in the fall and didn't see the results till spring. Then you put tiny seeds in the ground that wouldn't bear fruit until fall. You had to stick around in the meantime. A garden said to fate, "You can't get rid of me!"

Yes, she'd have a garden! Daffodils and tulips and pussy willows—*were* there such things anymore? She hadn't seen one since she was child. And forsythia. Great, cascading forsythia bushes along the whole west fence. And, in the fall, bronze and red chrysanthemums.

Thelma arrived in her Lincoln, which looked like a metallic gray galleon under full sail. Jane didn't hear her coming, and was surprised when Thelma caught her in the yard and said, "Aren't you worried about chiggers?"

Jane laughed. "I worry about a lot of things, but not chiggers. I was planning a garden."

"Oh, dear..."

"What?"

"Well, I know Steve wouldn't have liked it. He was so proud of his lawn." She scuffed a well-shod toe against a clump of crabgrass. The message was clear. Jane was desecrating his memory by her disregard for the lawn.

Steve's not around to know or care! Jane wanted to shout. But there was no point in getting this afternoon off to a worse start than absolutely necessary. So she ignored Thelma's comment and went on. "I'm going to dig up that section and have some vegetables. Corn and tomatoes and some beans to can."

"Jane, you wouldn't! Home-canned beans are the most common source of food poisoning there is."

"Oh, did you think I meant to eat them? No, no, no. I just meant to bottle them up for the county fair display."

"Jane, I don't find sarcasm very becoming in a woman. I'm sure Steve would have agreed with me."

"You'd be surprised—" She stopped, midsentence. "Never mind, Thelma. Let's go in. I need to stir the spaghetti sauce."

"How delightful. Spaghetti... again."

Fortunately, Thelma had pretty well lost interest in the murder next door. Except for expressing horror at being so close to the scene, she found that the subject deprived her of being the center of attention.

Ted's worry, naturally, was how it might adversely affect property values. "I want you to be able to get every penny you can out of this house, Jane," he said with genuine concern.

"I'm not planning to leave this house for centuries, Ted, and everyone will have forgotten about it long before then. But I appreciate your concern."

"Oh, I didn't mean to suggest that you should leave—"

"I know you didn't." She gave him a warm smile. Dear Ted, always so afraid he might upset her.

Dixie Lee simply didn't want to hear about "icky" things like dead bodies.

Uncle Jim, tucking into the spaghetti like he might never get another chance, kept a tactful silence. Jane was relieved that he made no reference to his familiarity with crime and criminals.

The subject only came up peripherally once more, as Thelma was leaving. She made a point of brushing furiously at some imaginary dust on the sleeve of the smart green linen jacket she'd worn. She glanced into the hall closet where it had hung, as if to determine just how filthy it really was.

"You really will have to have someone in, Jane, dear."

"I did. Day before yesterday."

"It's a pity one can't get good help these days. Why, when I was a girl, we had a houseful of servants, and they wouldn't have let a speck of dust collect."

No, you'd have probably given those poor, downtrodden souls twenty lashes, Jane thought.

"And they were just like part of the family. They knew all our little idiosyncrasies; how much starch to put in Papa's shirts, and how Mother liked her bath things laid out. And they knew things about we children that even our parents didn't know about. Oh, Jane dear, I almost forgot—"

She took a large white envelope from her purse and handed it to Jane.

Through gritted teeth, Jane said, "Thank you, Thelma."

Ted and Dixie Lee followed her out, and Jane's kids made their break for freedom; Katie and Mike to visit friends, Todd to ride bikes with Elliot Wallenberg on the playground lot. Uncle Jim made as if to join the exodus, but she put her hand on his arm and said, "Please stay a while."

"Something wrong?"

"No, I'd just like to visit with you, and there's never time with the gang around."

Jane poured two beers and went out to sit on the patio with him. A little breeze had sprung up, frightening Willard into trying to sit in Jane's lap. They chatted for a bit and eventually came around to the murder. Jane told him everything she knew, which was precious little, and finished up with a recounting of her conversation with Suzie Williams and the subsequent irritating brush with VanDyne.

"I don't imagine he meant to be insulting, Janey. He was probably sincere about you having a special insight. Most men would never have reason to know specialized things about how a house is run."

"But it was his manner that made me so mad."

"Speaking of manner, what was that frozen smile you gave old Thelma when she handed you that envelope? You didn't even open it. And it seems to happen every time we have dinner."

"It was my allowance," Jane said.

Uncle Jim sat forward, his look worried. "Honey, are you having money problems?"

"No, I have plenty. Well, not plenty, but enough, if I'm reasonably careful." Jim had alluded to her finances before, not out of nosiness, but concern. It was time she explained. "You know Thelma and her late husband had a pharmacy. Steve and Ted got degrees in pharmacology and business both and they opened the other two big drugstores with Thelma. That was about the time Steve and I got married, and I not only put in all my money—a small inheritance from my grandmother—but I worked at one of the stores for nearly a year without pay, just to help get it off the ground. Well, as Steve's widow, and because of what I put in, I own a third interest, and that envelope she gave me is my part of the profits."

"Then why call it your 'allowance'?"

"That's what it seems like. I know perfectly well it's my money and I'm entitled to it, but she hands it out like charity and, dammit, I accept it as such. She can't just mail the damned thing or give it to me privately. It's always a production, like a gift."

"I don't understand why you've got a third and Thelma has a third and she lives like it's a million a month?"

"Because I don't get all of mine. I had a trust set up for the kids; half of my share goes straight into it. And Thelma has a lot of other investments as well."

"Have you talked to Ted about all this? I think you should. He's a nice young man. I think he'd understand if you asked him to mail it to you himself."

"Dear Ted—all he thinks about is the business and Dixie Lee. But you may be right. I'll try it. I know he'll understand, it's just a question of whether he'll stand up to Thelma. He's wonderful at ignoring her, but a confrontation? I don't know."

They sat quietly. Meow came in from the field with a mouse, which she generously tried to give to Willard, who ran for cover under the foundation plantings. Jim finally said, "Honey, how *are* you getting along? Not money, just everything. Have you met any other men?"

"Good Lord, no! I haven't even thought about it."

"That's not right, Janey. I know you loved Steve, but he's gone and you—"

"Oh, Uncle Jim," she interrupted, her voice quavering over his concern. "You don't understand."

"It always seems like that, but I do, Janey. I've lost my own wife, remember."

Jane looked off into the yard, where next year there was going to be a fine garden. It was a day for revelations.

"Uncle Jim, haven't you ever wondered why Steve was out on the road at midnight on the coldest night in February?"

"A business trip, I guess. There was a suitcase in the car."

"Uncle Jim, he was leaving me."

Chapter Eleven

There was a long silence while he absorbed this. Jane, staring at a nonexistent bank of forsythia bushes, was thinking that if she said this enough times, maybe it would hurt less. The only other person she'd ever told was Shelley, and that was the night of the accident. It had been locked up inside her all this time, and by damn, it *did* feel good to say it to Uncle Jim. Like taking a pressure cooker off the burner.

"Janey, I had no idea. I'm sorry."

"So was I." Now that she'd started, no power on earth could have kept her from telling him the whole ugly thing. "Steve had come home late from the office—or somewhere—that night and told me he was in love with someone else. A married woman who was going to divorce her husband for him. I never even got the chance to weasel out of him who it was."

"The bastard," Jim said under his breath.

Jane heard him. "That's what I thought. When the highway patrolman told me about the accident, all I could think was, the son of a bitch deserved to die. Of course, that feeling passed. Well, sort of passed. Steve's death was a double whammy. I'd lost him twice in one hour. A lot of women are widowed. A lot are dumped. Few of us get it both in one night."

"Janey, why didn't you tell me things weren't right between you? Maybe I could have talked to him."

"I imagine I would have," she said, suspecting this was a lie, "but I didn't know, Uncle Jim. I honestly didn't know! I thought everything was fine. It was like being hit in the head with a sledgehammer when he told me. I

wasn't even mad or hurt right at first, just dumbfounded.
And—embarrassed. I felt like an absolute *fool*. I was still
pacing around my bedroom, crying and raging and wondering what in hell I was going to tell the kids, and
thinking somehow I could get him back, when the police
came to the door. Of course, I know now that I couldn't
have gotten him back and I wouldn't have wanted it that
way. I've never been much good at forgiveness."

"Janey, I'm so awfully sorry."

"Well, it has its bright spots, in a grim sort of way. If
he'd divorced me, I'd be living in poverty, probably.
Divorce settlements aren't very kind to wives with three
kids and no job skills these days. And what do I know how
to do? Drive car pools, give birthday parties, bandage
scraped knees? Not very useful when it comes to making a
living. The mortgage on the house had a life insurance
policy that paid it off. By dying before he could get rid of
me, Steve left me this house free and clear, and believe
me, you'd have to fire-bomb it to get me out!"

"He really was a bastard."

"No, he wasn't. Only at the last. He was a good
husband until he found somebody else. It's been long
enough now that I'm beginning to be able to look back and
see that. He always remembered special days and bought
thoughtful gifts. I loved him for good reason, Uncle Jim,"
she said, hating the tears that were running down her face
and unable to stop them. "And the kids did too. He was a
wonderful father. Never missed a Little League game or Boy
Scout camp-out. One time he cancelled an important
business trip because Katie had her first piano recital—
Oh, dear . . . you'd think I'd be better at crying after all the
practice I've had. Excuse me a minute, please."

She ran inside to collect herself. After some furious
nose-blowing, she washed her face, put on fresh makeup,
and returned to the patio. "Thanks for listening, Uncle
Jim," she said briskly. "Now, I need some cheese and
crackers to soak up the beer. How about you?"

"Sounds great, honey," he said, tactfully adopting her
attitude that everything was normal and the conversation
about Steve had never happened.

She fixed a snack and they talked, very deliberately,

of other things, most of them having to do with gardens, all of them innocuous. Willard, hoping the deadly mouse was gone, came skulking back. After a while, Jane's mind wandered back to the death of the cleaning lady.

"I've been thinking about what Thelma said about the servants when she was a girl—"

"All horseshit. I'll bet she grew up in a tar paper shack with waxed paper for windowpanes."

Jane laughed. "Don't I wish! No, what I meant was the stuff about servants knowing all about you. Didn't you hear what she said?"

"I'm sure I heard it, but I've gotten good at not paying attention to the woman. You might do well to learn that skill, you know."

"I know. But she did say something I've been thinking about. Just hear me out, Uncle Jim, and tell me if you think I'm crazy." She went on to tell him her suspicions about Edith having gotten into the mysteriously unlocked desk drawer.

"Suppose she wasn't trying to steal anything—if it was she who opened it—but was only snooping?"

Uncle Jim leaned back, propping his big feet on another patio chair. "Damned hard to prove, blackmail. It's one of the crimes that victims don't want to admit to. If you tell the police, or even a friend, that you're being blackmailed, they naturally want to know what for. I'll run her through the computer for you in the morning, though. Just to see what turns up. Of course, your Detective VanDyne has already done that, but he's not apt to share it with you."

"I'll say! Could you talk to him about it?"

"Nope. Out of my jurisdiction. If the township asks the metropolitan police for help, they get it. Otherwise, we stay out. Some police departments are real touchy about what they see as interference. I'll tell you one thing, though, honey, and you'd better pay attention."

"Yes, sir!" she said with a salute. But underneath the affectionate mockery, there was alarm. It was unlike him to speak so authoritatively to her.

"I don't want you to have that cleaning woman back here for any reason."

"Don't worry. Murder aside, I didn't like her. And I don't like even the suspicion that she was pawing through my belongings. The lady I had before wouldn't so much as open a drawer to get out a dish towel without asking me. I used to think it was a terrible nuisance, but now I'm beginning to see her as an angel. Don't worry, I won't let Edith back in the house."

"And you'll lock up real well?"

"I always do."

"No, you don't. I've been here three or four times that you were cooking and just yelled for me to come in."

"But that's when I'm home," Jane protested guiltily. She'd gotten very lax about keeping the house locked—until a few days earlier.

"When you're home is the only time you can be hurt at home," Uncle Jim pointed out sternly. "If you're going to leave the doors unlocked, you'd be better off to do it when you're gone than when you're here."

Jane lit a cigarette. "You think there's really a danger, then?"

He reached over and patted her arm. "I don't mean to scare you, honey. No. I don't think anybody's after you. But when somebody's been murdered a few yards away and the murderer hasn't been identified, well, it's only reasonable to be safe instead of sorry."

They sat quietly for a few minutes before Jim started stirring himself to depart. "Good dinner, Janey."

"I've got a doggie bag for you. Uncle Jim, do you ever eat real food?"

"Sure, every time I come here."

"Then come more often. Why do I have to drag you out to see me?"

"It's not you. I'd like to see you every day. It's this place. The suburbs. All this—space. And tidiness."

"Too wholesome for you?"

He laughed. "It's true, I guess. A place like this doesn't need a guy like me. I don't give a damn about grass, and if I had a yard, everything would die for sure. But in the city, there's always already a mess, a domestic disturbance, some slob I can try to straighten out. Sometimes I even do some good."

She walked him to his car by way of the kitchen and handed him two plastic containers with sauce and pasta and some foil-wrapped garlic bread. He set them on the floor of the front seat and gave her back the containers she'd sent stew and salad in the last time.

"Janey, would you like for me to come stay with you until this is sorted out?"

"I'd adore it, but I'd be overwhelmed with guilt at the amount of driving you'd have to do every day. You'd be on the road three hours a day. I've ridden with you, and I don't think the Chicago highway system is ready for that. Besides, you'd probably go raving mad within a day and I'd have to find a good mental institution to put you in. It would cut into my free time."

"I could get a policewoman or private detective agency to send someone..." he said, obviously relieved that she'd turned down his offer.

"That's all I need. A strange woman in the house. I've got a very strange one already who's beating down the doors to move in."

"Thelma? Don't you do it. The old bitch would chew you up and spit you out in a week. I'll call you tomorrow with whatever I find out about your nosy cleaning lady. And, speaking of nosy—"

"What?"

"Don't go interfering in this, Janey."

"What do you mean?"

"All this talk about what you and your friend Shelley have figured out, and the business about VanDyne not being willing to tell you anything—that kind of butting in could be dangerous too. All you need to know is how to be careful and keep yourself out of any possible danger. Ignorance can, and often is, safety."

"Then I ought to be about the most secure person in the world, Uncle Jim. There's hardly anything I don't know less than I should about. Keep an eye on that sauce or you'll have to shovel it off the floor of the car."

She smiled and waved as he drove off, but when she went in the house, she grimly checked that the doors were all locked. She'd have to make sure the kids all had keys tomorrow and impress upon them, without being too scary, that they had to keep the house safe.

Chapter Twelve

There was neither band practice nor cheerleader practice on Monday mornings, a small kindness Jane was sure the school board was unaware of or they would have promptly corrected it. She was able to get up at the usual time and still make a big breakfast. The kids were dumbfounded.

"You don't mean we have to eat all this, do you?" Katie's nose wrinkled.

"Why not?"

"I couldn't walk around with all this stuff in my stomach. I'd feel like a balloon."

Mike's reaction was cautious curiosity. "What's this stuff?"

"An omelet with bacon and sliced onions and peppers."

"In the *morning*? God, Mom! If I blew into my tuba with that kinda breath, I'd never get rid of the smell. Nothing personal, Mom, but it looks like barf, besides. Sorry."

It was Todd who put it all into perspective. He silently studied the omelet, the orange juice, the English muffins, the Canadian bacon, and said, "What's wrong, Mom?"

That was, of course, why she'd done it. She knew they weren't breakfast-eaters. Back in her "good mother" stage she'd cooked a hundred breakfasts that were rejected. She'd only done it today because she was scared. She had a sudden sense of how short life can be and how unexpectedly it can end. Now that she thought about it, the last time she'd gone on a breakfast binge was in the month after

Steve died. What was it in her that fended off death and destruction with breakfasts? Send them to heaven on a full stomach? Good nutrition fends off the grim reaper?

When she had them on their way, she phoned Shelley. "Wanna come have four breakfasts with me?"

"Love to, but I can't. I've got to jump in the shower, then I've got a dozen errands to do. Want to ride along for the first round?"

"Sure. I'll eat a barfy omelet while you're showering."

Katie was right about starting the day like a balloon. By the time Jane heard Shelley in her driveway, she felt like she could have just tucked in her arms and legs and rolled across to Nowack's.

"What are we shopping for?" she asked, hoisting herself into Shelley's minivan.

"Shopping center to return some bath towels."

As soon as they got out of the subdivision and onto a main road, Jane said, "Shelley, I've been thinking about that woman getting killed..."

"What about it?" Shelley said, frowning and braking as a little green sports car cut viciously in front of her. "Silly jerk. Doesn't he know if I hit him in this thing I'm all right, but he's catmeat?"

"Two things. First, I realized something when I went to the Little League game. I sat by Suzie Williams—"

"Learn any new words?" Shelley said, grinning.

"Not this time. Listen. A bunch of the kids ran into each other and one of them came limping off the field and Suzie thought it was her little boy. She got clear down the bleachers before she realized it was another kid. She came back and said something about all of them looking alike in their uniforms."

She paused, letting the thought soak in to Shelley's traffic-fuddled brain. She was easing the minivan into a parking place near the main entrance to the shopping center. They didn't talk until they were inside. "Damn! I thought Marshall Fields was at this end. We've got to walk clear down the mall," Shelley said.

They set out briskly, passing an endless number of shoe stores. "Have you ever noticed that nobody's ever actually buying shoes in these places?" Jane mused. Eyes on the shop window they were passing, she collided with a solid bank of elderly men taking their daily health-walk. Shelley stood aside while Jane extricated herself from canes and walkers and apologized. She had no sooner gotten free when, from the other direction, four women outfitted in stylish jogging suits and wearing fanatically determined expressions nearly ran her down.

"When did the mall become a running track?" Jane complained. "What happened to leisurely strolling?"

Shelley made no comment. She'd apparently been brooding over what Jane had been saying in the car. "So you figure whoever killed Ramona meant to kill Edith and mistook her?" she asked, resuming her quick pace. "But Jane, they don't look that much alike."

Jane tried to answer without panting. "But you vacuum with your back to the doorway."

No explanation was necessary. Shelley accepted this and went on. "But why? So what if it was supposed to be Edith instead of Ramona? That doesn't get you any closer to knowing who or why. Have you told Detective VanDyne about this idea?"

They'd come to an escalator, and Jane was able to get her breath for a moment. "Oh, I have. I'll tell you how charming he was about vacuuming backwards later. As a matter of fact, the idea had occurred to him as well."

"And did he think it was meant to be Edith?"

"He didn't share his thoughts," Jane replied archly.

Shelley arched an eyebrow, but didn't ask for an elaboration. They reached the other end of the mall, and Jane occupied herself studying all the pretty linens on sale while Shelley managed her towel return. Jane had been witness to some of Shelley's transactions before, and it wasn't always a pretty sight. What Shelley wanted, she got, no matter how many broken bodies were left behind in the process.

The thought made her uneasy. It wasn't that she suspected her friend of having anything to do with the murder of the cleaning lady. Shelley could no more kill someone than *she* could. But still . . . her mind kept involuntarily coming back to her, and she kept shaking off her suspicions as fast as they formed.

"There. All taken care of," Shelley announced.

"Where next?" Jane asked as they returned at break-neck pace to the van.

"The feedstore, for birdseed."

"Feedstore? You've got to be kidding? Are there such things around here?" Someone had parked so close to the minivan that Jane could hardly open the door and squeeze in.

"Not on every corner, but I found one. It's not far."

"Why don't you just buy birdseed at the grocery store?"

"That junk? That's for people who don't know birds. I have a special combination I mix myself. Are you in? Good. Now, you were saying about VanDyne? . . ." She pulled into traffic.

Jane told her about the conversation she'd had with him, but finished by saying, "Forget about him for a minute. I want to tell you why somebody wanted to kill Edith." The idea was only partially developed in her own mind, but she needed to hear herself say it before she'd know whether it had any merit. "Remember the talk we had on the phone about my desk drawer being meddled with? Well, I think that's the other part of the story. I think Edith had gone snooping in it. You see, we were trying to figure out who would want to steal anything in it. What we didn't consider was somebody wanting to steal information."

They'd reached a dilapidated shopping center in a suburb that looked like it had once been a little outlying town before Chicago oozed out and engulfed it. Shelley circled around a dry cleaner of questionable hygiene and went down an alley. There, looking like a scrap of country town, was a clapboard building that had big bags of fertilizer and grass seed piled in front and a faded sign that said, *FEED*.

"What in the world are you talking about?" Shelley asked, coming to a stop in front of this vision and turning the engine off. "This is all too baroque for me."

"Blackmail."

"Blackmail! You?"

Jane bristled. "I'm certain she was quite disappointed in her efforts to find out anything interesting about me."

"Oh, I didn't mean that. Well, maybe I did."

Jane smiled. "I guess I might as well just face the fact that I'm boring and be proud of it. A few more encounters with Detective VanDyne ought to do the trick."

"Jane, we're both boring in a conventional sense. All of us are. But blackmail? And how does my missing pearl necklace figure in this theory?"

"Beats me," Jane said. "It might not have anything to do with it. The necklace might have been missing for a while, mightn't it? When were you last sure you had it?"

"The day I stuck it in the drawer a year or so ago," Shelley admitted. "Let me think about this while I get the birdseed."

She hadn't been kidding about her recipe for birdseed. She took in two big, empty, lidded plastic buckets that had once contained a stupendous amount of plaster, and had the clerk fill them with a precise mixture of shelled sunflower seeds ("The cardinals love it."), shelled peanuts ("For chickadees."), safflower seeds ("A favorite with the titmice") and cracked corn ("Sparrows have to eat something.")

While Shelley supervised the mixing, Jane roamed around the store. It was like being in a different world, a rather old world. Or at least an unfamiliar one to a woman who had lived nearly everywhere on earth but the American farm belt. Besides the barrels of every seed known to the mind of man or bird, there were barrels of rabbit food—which looked surprisingly like rabbit droppings—and pressed-meal dog bones big enough for a woolly-mammoth-sized dog. There were all sorts of cages and water troughs and animal food dispensers, and a huge supply of old-fashioned mousetraps. There were even salt licks for deer. In another section, she found canning equipment, heavy ceramic bowls, and blue-speckled pots and pans and giant coffee pots, like cowboys probably had on the trail.

On the last aisle there were gardening supplies. This evidence of suburbia was probably what kept the delightfully old-fashioned store in business. Here, the floor had been cleared, and a big sign said that in a short time this section would be full of the best quality Dutch bulbs for fall planting. Next to the sign, a wire rack contained a tidy stack of bulb catalogues. Jane picked one up and was paying for it when Shelley's long-suffering clerk went staggering out the door under the substantial weight of her purchases.

"We can always tell autumn is just around the corner when you come in, Miz Nowack," he was saying as Jane got in the minivan. "You're always the first to stock up."

"Everybody feeds the birds in the winter, and if I start earlier I get all the good ones," Shelley replied with a laugh as she started the van.

She shifted conversational gears as easily as the van's gears. They'd hardly cleared the driveway of the feed store when she said, "In some ways it makes sense, Jane. If you leave the pearls out of it. One thing it would explain is the difference in the way people feel about Edith. You know— some people who are fanatically clean swear by her, and others who are slobs didn't think she did a good job."

"I don't quite—"

"See, if you're a terrific housekeeper and you're being blackmailed by her, it would be dangerous to bad-mouth her, so you'd claim she was good even if you knew she was awful."

"And you'd have to keep her on because, if you fired her, she'd tell people. No. That's backwards. If she's getting money from you for blackmail, she doesn't need to work for you anymore, but if you fire her, how can you go around saying how good she is? My brain is turning to mush."

"Hmmm," Shelley mused. "You've got a point. There are two ways of looking at this. Who's being blackmailed? The ones who keep her or the ones who fire her? Either way, if you keep her or not, you'd be under orders from her not to criticize, because the only way she has of getting a supply of new victims is to keep having new homes opened to her. Good God, Jane! What's happening to us? Here we are, inventing this whole ugly little scenario with details and finishing touches—just on the strength of your thinking maybe someone got into your desk."

"But you believe it, don't you?"

"Yes, I'm afraid I do. At least it's one way of accounting for what happened, and so far nothing else has made the least bit of sense."

They were quiet as Shelley negotiated an entrance ramp onto the highway. Finally, as they neared their street, Shelley said, "You know what this all means, if we accept it?"

"What?"

"That poor old Ramona Thurgood was killed by a woman, and by a woman we know."

"Shelley! What a thing to say!"

"Think about it. We know everybody Edith works for. Monday she does Joyce Greenway. Tuesday is Mary Ellen Revere, and Wednesday is Robbie Jones—or maybe it's the other way around. Then Thursday is me, and Friday is you."

"Not anymore. Besides, she's worked for lots of other people. You said yourself it could be that she doesn't go on working for the people she's blackmailing."

"Still, she's a sort of fixture in the neighborhood. Look how many people we know who have had her clean for them at one time or another. Besides, if it had been somebody we don't know who killed her, then how would they have found out she would be at my house on Thursday? I don't think the Happy Helper people give out that kind of information. In fact, I know they don't. I had a woman from there once when our usual lady was on vacation a year or so ago, and she left her watch by the sink. When she didn't call me to say she'd left it by the next day, I phoned the company to find out if I could just drop it off to her if she was in the neighborhood. The company sent a guy out in a truck to pick it up instead of telling me where to find her."

"I still think there must have been some other way. Suppose she mentioned working for you to some other customer? Some stranger."

"And just incidentally told them which day she worked for me, what my address is—remember, we're not listed in the phone book—and which week she was supposed to be n my house alone? If you can buy that, I have a bridge in Brooklyn I'd like to tell you about."

"Oh," Jane said and subsided into silence until they pulled into Shelley's driveway. "You're saying, then, that if we accept this theory, one of our friends is not only being blackmailed, but is a murderer besides—"

"Friends, or acquaintances. I think the distinction may be important to us someday."

"And it's only somebody who knew she'd be there alone because you were going out to the airport for most of the day."

"Right."

"So who did you tell?"

"Everybody who was supposed to come to the meeting that night."

"Oh, Shelley, those people are all *really* friends of ours!"

"Afraid so. Jane, next time I go for birdseed, you'll understand why I don't invite you along for conversation," Shelley said grimly.

Chapter Thirteen

Shelley dropped off the birdseed and Jane and went off to do the rest of her errands. Jane, shaken badly by the result of her own chain of reasoning, sat down at the kitchen table with a cup of coffee and a cigarette.

She really ought to be doing something worthwhile. Ironing, laundry, or something, but she felt oddly drained. Thinking she could take her mind off murder, she flipped on the little black-and-white TV on the kitchen counter.

A group of extremely aggressive-looking women were presenting their theory that the society of the United States was rotten to the core. Their proof was that as members of a Communist-lesbian support group, they'd been denied the right to adopt children. Phil Donahue was weaving in and around the audience, attempting to make those who expressed even the mildest disagreement look like right-wing fanatics who might have been out burning crosses that very week.

Jane flipped the TV off, brooding. It was amazing what some people were eager to tell about themselves, eager to the point of wanting to share it with a national audience. She rather suspected that if she herself were a lesbian, a Communist, *or* someone who'd been passed over as unfit to be an adoptive parent, she'd probably want to keep the whole thing as quiet as possible. To be all three and want to tell the world about it amazed her.

Which brought her right back to the subject she was trying to avoid—Ramona Thurgood's murder. If she and Shelley were right in their reasoning, then someone they knew had a deep, dark secret. Not a secret to share with the public, but something so awful that she was willing to actually kill another human being to keep it quiet.

That one mental statement was crammed with considerations with which Jane was hardly prepared to cope. The fact that a woman could commit murder, for starters. Even though the news was filled with reports of women who killed, Jane could never quite bring herself to believe it. Murder was, to her, a strictly male activity. Being a mother, she was convinced that any mother could and would do anything to protect her children, but not necessarily herself. Very rarely herself. Stretching her imagination, she could just barely conceive of a few women she'd known *commissioning* a murder. Wanting it done so badly they'd have it done secondhand. That, of course, raised the question of how one found somebody to commit murder for you, but that didn't seem to be the point here.

Besides, what secret could be so dark and dangerous and compelling? After all, these were people she *knew*. Of course, everybody had something they didn't want others to know about—well, everybody except the people who wanted to be on Phil Donahue's show. Even though Jane's life abroad had prepared her for many things, she wasn't at all prepared to picture her neighbors, who belonged to the PTA, as people capable of having done something so awful that they might turn to murder.

A knock at the kitchen door startled her. She suddenly remembered that, in spite of her resolve, she had failed to lock it. Uncle Jim was right. She had ridiculously careless habits. Peering through the curtains, she saw with relief that it was Shelley.

"Come in. I thought you had errands to do."

"I do, but I couldn't do them for thinking about all this," Shelley admitted. "I was supposed to pick up the dog, but I just couldn't face having him hang on my pant cuffs. I'm going to leave him at the kennel till the kids get home. Jane, I want this settled so the kids *can* come home. I miss them, but I won't have them back until I know we're all safe—at least from whoever killed that woman. Jane, I've got to get all that stuff out of the refrigerator and the dishes back to people. Come help me clean it out, will you?"

"Sure. Let me get my keys." As she was reaching for her purse, the phone rang and she grabbed it. "Hello?"

"Mrs. Jeffry? This is Karen from the Specialty Siding Company. We have a crew in your neighborhood giving estimates this week. You do own your own home there at—"

"Do you?"

"Do I what?"

"Do you own your own home?"

There was the usual baffled silence at the other end of the line. Jane smiled smugly. It always worked.

"I—well, that is to say, I don't quite understand—"

"You're trying to tell me it's none of my business, aren't you?" Jane interrupted warmly. "Well, it's none of your business either. Good-bye."

"Roofing and siding?" Shelley asked. "That's clever. I usually just lie and tell them I rent."

"That works?"

"Yup. They only want to talk to somebody who can commit their very own thousands of dollars to covering up the outside of the house. I like yours better. It gets closer to the heart of why those calls make me so mad."

"Do you suppose most people tell them the truth without a fight?" Jane asked as they went outside. She locked the kitchen door and tested it to make sure it latched.

"They must or they wouldn't keep asking."

"I've been thinking about it . . ." As they went to Shelley's house, Jane told her about the Donahue show. "We're being conditioned to tell anybody who asks us anything they want to know. Like the so-called survey calls that ask you one stupid question about a television show, then your age and income, and proceed to try to sell you four thousand magazines you don't want for twice what it would normally cost. But at the same time most people are spilling their guts to anybody who asks, some people are hoarding pretty awful secrets."

They sat down at the kitchen table. Shelley had been clipping grocery store coupons and started gathering them up and putting them into the small cardboard file she kept in her purse. "Here's one for cat food I saved for you," she said.

Jane folded it and stuffed it in her jeans pocket. She was still brooding over secrets told and secrets kept. "Do you have any awful secrets, Shelley? I don't mean I'm asking what they are, just if you have any."

"You know them all," Shelley said. "Except for some stupid, embarrassing things, most of which I've mercifully forgotten."

"My secrets are petty in the world's scheme of things," Jane said. "Once I forgot to pay for a loaf of bread at a market in France, and deliberately didn't go back to pay when I realized it. My worst was chipping a tiny flake of rock off one of the stones at Stonehenge. I was dared on a school outing. I felt horrible about it for months, and tried to figure out how I could send it back, but I was only twelve and I was scared that they'd get my fingerprints off the envelope and trace me to my father and he'd lose his job in the State Department for having such a wicked daughter."

"My worst was shoplifting a bikini. I must have been about sixteen, and of course my mother wouldn't give me the money to buy a thing like that, so, in desperation, I stole it. Of course, then I was faced not only with the guilt, but with the knowledge that I didn't ever dare wear it."

"But Shelley, those are stupid things that all kids do in some variation. Not grown-up, horrible secrets."

"Well, you do have one grown-up, horrible secret..."

"You mean about Steve and whoever the bitch was? Even that doesn't really qualify. I couldn't be blackmailed about it. It's not something awful I did. Just something that would make me feel embarrassed if people knew. I certainly wouldn't kill anybody to keep it quiet."

Shelley's phone rang. "Yes? Oh, hello, Detective VanDyne. Yes, that would be fine. Yes, she's right here with me. I'll ask. Jane, could you stay here for a while? Yes, that's fine. Ten minutes, then."

She hung up and said, "He wants to tell me how things are coming along and double check with you about the times you saw people coming and going. He'll be right over.

"Oh, God! I look like I've been pulled through a knothole!"

"I thought you didn't like him?"

"I didn't like him thinking I was a frumpy housewife and I'm sitting here the living proof of it!"

"You've got time to run home. Put on that cherry sweater you bought last week."

"Not the green one with the navy trim?"

Shelley paused a moment, then grinned. "Jane, I wouldn't be your friend if I continued to keep this from you. That green sweater makes you look like you just gave six quarts of blood."

Jane laughed. "That must be why people are always so solicitous when I wear it. Always asking how I feel."

She made it just moments before the detective, and was sitting calmly at the kitchen table wearing the cherry sweater and crisp, black slacks when his MG purred to a stop in the driveway. Shelley had been on the phone when she returned and was still talking. Jane had the impression she was talking to Paul, but wasn't sure. As the doorbell rang, Shelley said, "Right, honey. Thanks for telling me. I *was* worried. Bye-bye." She hung up and said quickly, "Jane, don't mention those pearls to VanDyne. I know who took them."

"Who—?"

"Please, come in," Shelley was saying to the detective.

Jane studied him as Shelley invited him in and fixed him a cup of coffee and a plate of cookies. He was just as good-looking as Jane remembered. He was probably a few years younger than she, but, according to the gossip columns, that didn't matter these days. She wondered briefly what sort of money he made, but then quickly reminded herself she wasn't looking for someone to marry, just someone to date occasionally.

Maybe.

She hadn't been on a date since she met Steve. Eighteen years ago! What did people do on dates these days? She was pretty sure the old kiss-on-the-third-date rule didn't apply, but did everybody just hop into bed with everyone now? Oh, dear. That would put her at a real disadvantage. She'd be a Victorian in a time warp. Imagine letting someone you hadn't known intimately for years see your stretch marks. Horrors! Besides, if she ever did go out with somebody like this, the fun of it would be in being seen with him. And then there were the kids to consider . . .

"Mrs. Jeffry?"

She had the feeling he'd spoken to her more than once. "Sorry, I was just thinking about—something."

"I know this must be very upsetting to you both," he said.

Let him think it was murder on her mind, not sex. "Of course. But you must call me Jane. 'Mrs. Jeffry' makes me feel very old."

"Okay," he said with a charming smile, but he didn't offer his first name. "And you're Shelley, aren't you?"

"Yes," Shelley answered, but the look in her eyes said, "Mrs. Nowack to you, buddy."

Oh, dear. If Shelley had taken a dislike to him, Jane figured she'd better give up on him. It wouldn't be a bit of fun giggling girlishly over a conquest that your friend didn't approve of. "Now, what did you want to talk to me about?" she asked him.

"First, I wanted to fill Mrs. Nowack in on what we've learned."

So he had caught that expression and duly noted it. Good for him.

"Mrs. Jeffry suggested that the regular cleaning woman probably was the intended target. That's simply a theory, of course. She has no proof. But it is something to consider and discard—"

"Discard!" Jane exclaimed. "You know perfectly well there's absolutely nothing questionable about Mrs. Thurgood's past. Unless you're lying to us and the newspapers about her. Are you?"

"Why would we need to do that?"

"And you know by now what mixed reviews Edith gets," she went on.

"Mixed reviews?"

"Some of our friends who are very good housekeepers think the world of her," Shelley explained, "and others who are . . . well, slobs, to be honest, didn't think she did a very good job."

"And which are you, Mrs. Nowack?"

"She's only worked for me once and I didn't think she did a very good job."

"And you?" he asked Jane. "I understand she was at your house the day after the murder."

"I'm one of the slobs who didn't think she did a terribly good job," Jane replied honestly. "I mean, she did the minimum well enough, but no more." He hadn't admitted that her theory had any merit, but at least he was asking questions about Edith. Certainly that meant he was coming around to her way of thinking.

"What conclusions do you draw from this discrepancy?" he asked.

"What an odd question," Shelley said. "Why should our conclusions matter? It's yours that count. What do you think—or aren't you allowed to say?"

That put him in an obviously uncomfortable position. He stirred his coffee, cocking his head at her as if considering how much he ought to say. The silence grew longer, and Shelley's original animosity seemed to be growing.

Jane—wisely or not—took matters in her own hands. "I can't speak for anybody, but I think she was blackmailing customers—or ex-customers. I haven't figured out which."

"Why do you think that?" His tone was pleasant. Almost amused. Or did Jane just imagine a patronizing tone?

"Because the one time she did work for me, I believe she broke into a locked drawer in a room I asked her not to go into."

She was rewarded with a smile. A genuine, dimple-flashing smile. She nearly slipped off her chair.

"Tell me more about it," he said.

Jane did. She tried to go easy on the domestic aspects of glasses repair kits and files of report cards and envelopes with baby teeth the tooth fairy had bought. He listened in silence.

"So nothing was missing, but you're sure the contents were disturbed?"

"Fairly sure. But there's no proof."

"We could fingerprint the drawer, but you probably smudged any that might have been there."

"Sorry," Jane said automatically.

"It's all right. It wouldn't have proved anything anyway. Just confirmation of your suspicion. By the way, you might be interested in knowing that Edith isn't doing any of her jobs this week. She called in and said she was having a bad spell with a wisdom tooth."

"Ahh, so you think she's figured the same thing and is scared?" Jane asked.

He acted as if he hadn't heard the question. Turning his attention back to Shelley, who'd started tapping her spoon lightly on the table while staring thoughtfully out the kitchen door, he said, "We've checked on all the service vehicles seen that day in the neighborhood. All were legitimate. Furniture deliveries, plumbing repairs, and so forth. There were also three people seen walking the block that we know of. One was a woman collecting for charity, another was an insurance adjuster working a fire-damage claim, and the third was a paper boy home from school with chicken pox, but out making his collections. All of them were exactly what they claimed to be. The only other people known to be near this house were the ladies who brought the food."

He left it at that for the moment, giving them time to draw the obvious conclusion.

In an intellectual way, Jane was gratified to have her own suspicions confirmed. At the same time, she felt her heart constrict. It was one thing to jabber about something like this with Shelley; it was altogether a different matter when an officer of the law all but told them one of their acquaintances was a potential murderer. She wanted badly to go back to the old wandering-maniac theory.

In spite of the cherry sweater and the bright shaft of sunlight coming through Shelley's sparkling windows, Jane began to shiver. This wasn't a game and it didn't matter if VanDyne liked them or not. He had to know the truth. "Shelley, tell him about the pearls."

"No, Jane."

"What pearls?" VanDyne asked.

"Shelley had a strand of pearls that were stolen," Jane said. "She didn't want you to know because she didn't want her husband to know they were gone."

"Jane, I wish you hadn't said that. I told you I knew who took the pearls."

"Who?"

"Paul."

Chapter Fourteen

"Your husband stole your pearls?" VanDyne asked.

"Technically, they are his and no, he didn't steal them. He took them—to be cleaned and appraised," Shelley explained. She was actually blushing, something Jane had never seen happen. "I told Jane earlier I was supposed to have put them in the safe-deposit box and I didn't. I discovered after the murder that they were missing, and I didn't want my husband to know I hadn't taken care of them."

"That's why you didn't tell me when I asked if anything was missing?" VanDyne asked. He was a little curt. Almost disgusted.

"Because of that and because I had no idea when they disappeared. They could have been gone for a year. Jane, that's what Paul was calling about a few minutes ago. I guess I kept staring at that drawer, and he noticed. He called to tell me not to worry."

"Were they real?" Jane asked.

"No. High-grade fakes, though. With some value just because they're good antique imitations."

"I beg your pardon, ladies. But is this really pertinent?" VanDyne asked.

"It is to me," Shelley replied sharply.

After a long pause, he bent and picked up a briefcase and removed a stack of papers. "Now, I'd like to go over these statements with you—"

"Statements?" Jane asked.

"From the women who came here that day. You were a witness to some of them arriving."

"I've already told you everything I know."

"Yes, but I thought going over it might help you remember more. Something insignificant you didn't think to tell us maybe? Now, I spoke to Mrs. Williams last night—"

Something about the awestruck tone in his voice when he mentioned Suzie's name made Jane and Shelley both smile. "Did you learn any new words?" Shelley asked.

"A few," he admitted. "She's quite a woman, isn't she?" There was both admiration and something like fear in the statement. "She says she's a buyer for the local branch of Marshall Fields."

"Lingerie and foundations, as I suppose she told you," Shelley said.

"Yes—ah, well, uh. Now, Mrs. Williams says she forgot to bring her dish over before she went to work, so she took an early lunch hour and ran home and then over here. She thinks that was about eleven."

"I wouldn't know," Jane said. "I was out shopping from around ten to about twelve."

"She told me Edith had cleaned her house once, but that she didn't like her. Do you know anything about that?"

"Nothing, except that's what she told me too."

"Oh, you've discussed this with her?"

"At a ball game Saturday. In fact, she's the one who first gave me the idea that it might be the wrong cleaning lady who was killed."

"She suggested that?" he asked, his eyes narrowing.

"No, she was talking about the boys in their uniforms and said all the cute little bastards looked alike in them."

"Yes, I imagine that *is* how she'd put it. Now, Mary Ellen Revere, your neighbor across the street. She said she came over just after that. She saw Mrs. Williams leaving and that reminded her to bring over her food."

Jane shrugged. "I don't know."

"She says she works at home except on Wednesdays, when she goes into the city for a weekly meeting with her other investors."

"I've never known what it is she does, but I see her

leaving in city clothes from time to time," Jane said. "What *is* it she does, exactly?"

"It's odd that you wouldn't know. All of you seem to know so much about each other."

"She doesn't have children," Shelley said. At his perplexed look, she elaborated. "Most of us know each other through our children. School things, sports, swimming pool, car pools to various activities. We only know Mary Ellen because she lives so close. When we have adult neighborhood parties we invite the Reveres, of course. They don't usually stick it out to the end, though."

"Antisocial?"

"No, but conversation eventually gets around to the kids' teachers and teams and baby-sitters and such and, naturally, that bores them."

"I see," he said, as if being instructed in some esoteric habits of a foreign country and finding them excessively tedious. "Mrs. Revere said she wasn't out of the house anytime except to bring—" he consulted his notes "—potato salad over here. Would you know anything to the contrary or anything that would confirm that?" He looked from Shelley to Jane.

"No, except that I know she wasn't feeling well. She's just broken her arm and it's very painful. I didn't ask, but I assume she can't drive, so she's probably stranded," Jane said. "I hadn't thought about that. I guess I ought to offer to take her to the store or something, but I imagine her husband's taking care of all that."

VanDyne was looking away, waiting for her to get over this little outburst of suburban trivia. "Now, Mrs. Wallenberg says she brought a cake over and you brought it in. You confirmed that the first time we talked. Did you see her again the rest of the day?"

"Not until after—after Mrs. Thurgood was killed. I phoned her as soon as we discovered the body and came back here. She picked my son up from school and dropped him off home after dinner. Come to think of it, I didn't see her then."

"She said she was playing tennis—all day." It was clear that he found this hard to believe.

"I'm certain she was. Dorothy lives for it. She was a

pro or almost a pro when she was young, and she married a man who's a sporting goods distributor. She's also a nurse, and does part-time volunteer work in a birth control clinic."

"Yes, she told me that. She said she'd had Edith clean for her once and didn't like her. Is she one of—well, you called them 'slobs'?"

"I'll say," Shelley put in. She'd been quiet for quite a while, but now she became talkative about Easter eggs in sofa cushions and elicited the dimpled smile again.

"Mrs. Jones said she brought her dish a little after noon. But you didn't see her?"

There was a note of skepticism in this that Jane found irritating. "Believe it or not, I really don't spend my days spying on Shelley's driveway. I was probably down looking at the furnace then."

"I see. Looking at the furnace. Mrs. Jones said she saw you earlier in the day."

"At the dry cleaners," Jane said curtly. Why couldn't it have been at a travel agency where she was picking up tickets for an exotic trip, or at a jeweler having a diamond necklace clasp fixed—at the very least a health club? The man would think she never went anywhere interesting. Unfortunately, it was true.

He waited to see if she'd go on. When she didn't, he said, "Let's see who else—Laura Stapler, the woman next door to Mrs. Nowack's on the other side. She says she brought her salad over around one-thirty and spoke to you?"

"I think it was a little bit before that. Ten or fifteen minutes, probably. I started the carrots at one and—" She was about to do it again, gab about telling time by carrot cookedness.

"You didn't start the carrots until that *afternoon?*" Shelley interrupted.

"I didn't see her leave, though," Jane went on hurriedly. "I was leaving when she came. She must have been the last one in the house. Let's see—" Jane got up and opened the refrigerator door. "Shelley, you haven't moved any of this since then, have you?"

"Well, I—the kids aren't home and we ate out—"

"I'm not accusing you of keeping a piggy kitchen. I just wonder if you got these potluck dishes out of order. Isn't this Laura's bowl on the top of the stack?"

She shut the door and thought a minute. "That doesn't matter. I mean, it doesn't tell us anything that's necessary to know."

"Why not? I thought it sounded good," VanDyne said, looking like he hated to admit it.

"The dishwasher was still on prewash when I came over after Shelley called. So Mrs. Thurgood must have started it just before she was killed, and everybody had come and gone before then."

VanDyne got up and looked at the controls of the dishwasher. "Mrs. Nowack, had you set this to start in the afternoon?"

"What do you mean? Oh, yes, it *is* one of those, isn't it?"

"One of what?" Jane asked, joining him and bending over to see what he was looking at. "What in the world *are* all these buttons, Shelley?"

"It's got a thing where you can load it up and program it to start in the middle of the night."

"Why in the world would anybody want to do that?" Jane asked.

"I have no idea. It would scare the stuffing out of me if it started gushing and thrashing at four A.M., so I never bothered to learn anything but 'wash' and 'cancel.'"

"It's so you can use it at nonpeak water consumption hours," VanDyne explained. "In some parts of the country that matters."

"So—" Jane began.

"So we've been looking at this dishwasher business as proof she was alive and it isn't necessarily. You're sure you didn't set it yourself, Mrs. Nowack?"

"Not unless I did it accidentally. I don't know or care how that timer gadget works."

"Wait a minute!" Jane said. "Don't you have a pathologist or coroner or somebody who can tell when she died?"

"Yes, but he can't set a very good time in this case. You see, that's determined in large part by the temperature of the body in relation to weight, room temperature, and the stage of rigor mortis, which is also influenced by surrounding temperature. That was a guest room, which Mrs. Nowack keeps closed off with the furnace vents also closed. It was pretty chilly the night before, so the room might have been quite cool. We don't know. When Mrs. Thurgood opened the door, she let it start warming up from who knows what temperature. In addition, the body was lying in a shaft of sunlight, which also threw off the temperature calculations. The coroner puts a tentative time of death at between noon and two. So, you see, the dishwasher evidence was in contradiction to that, and now we know—or suspect—why."

"You're saying whoever killed her very calmly set the dishwasher to start at a time when she—or he—had an alibi?"

"Not necessarily. It might have just been a last-minute gesture to generally confuse the issue. And it has."

Jane sat down shakily. She hadn't adjusted to the idea of one of her neighbors killing someone, much less doing it cold-bloodedly enough to think of something like that.

"Did any of the women who brought food see the cleaning lady when they came?" Shelley asked.

"Mrs. Wallenberg didn't, of course, because she was here before Mrs. Thurgood and didn't come in anyway. Mrs. Williams says the house was quiet, and so does Mrs. Revere, who came right after her. But Mrs. Jones was here an hour after that, and she mentioned that the victim was vacuuming the living room. Mrs. Greenway heard her moving around in the study. Mrs. Stapler says she didn't see or hear anything, but she also made the point that she stayed only briefly."

"Terrified, no doubt, even though she had no way of knowing anything was wrong. She's like that," Jane said. "Her husband has a safety store, whatever that is, and she takes caution very much to heart."

"Well, I guess that pretty well covers everybody who was in and out that day," Shelley said, leaning back.

VanDyne didn't reply for a minute; then he said, very softly, "Not quite everybody."

Jane thought for a second that he meant Shelley's

alibi hadn't held up. She knew she'd come to Shelley's defense, no matter what questions she might privately entertain.

He turned his head slightly, and Jane felt his gaze on her face.

"You *were* the last person to bring a dish, weren't you, Mrs. Jeffry?"

Chapter Fifteen

"That son of a bitch actually thinks I killed your cleaning lady!"

"Now, Jane. He doesn't either. You're overreacting."

They stood at the kitchen door, watching the red MG back out and drive away.

"Then why did he make that remark about my being the last person to bring a dish? And did you see the fishy look that went with it? The idiot was waiting for me to break down and confess, like the last scene in a Perry Mason movie!"

"Maybe he does suspect both of us," Shelley admitted. "But why shouldn't he? He doesn't know us any more than he knows the rest of them. Once you accept the premise that a perfectly respectable suburban housewife might have cold-bloodedly murdered somebody, where do you draw the line as to which one is capable of it?"

Jane sat down at the table. "It was bad enough being afraid of the killer, but now we have to be scared of the police too. They're supposed to look after dull, law-abiding people like us, not terrorize us."

"I know what you mean and I feel the same way, but I don't think he means to scare us. Asking questions about what you saw and heard is probably necessary information to clear you."

"This is when you start telling me about that bridge in Brooklyn you have for sale, right? Come on, Shelley!"

Shelley shrugged. "I don't see what we can do about it. As far as I'm concerned, VanDyne can suspect us all he wants. He's obviously not going to prove anything because we didn't do it. Here, help me get this stuff out of the refrigerator. That'll take your mind off him. I wonder if I ought to give the food back or not? This is Monday and it came on Thursday. No, it's probably going yucky. I think I'll run it all down the disposal and let everybody think Paul and I were pigs and ate it."

Jane got up and started handing bowls to Shelley. The first to go was her carrot salad. "I never even got to taste it," she said sadly. "I'm still mad, Shelley. If he really just wanted to clear me, he could have said so."

She handed over Laura's cucumber and onion salad; Shelley peeled off the plastic wrap and sniffed at the dish. "I love this stuff. What a pity to throw it out. Do you think—?"

"No, pitch it! This is the one that will really break your heart. The brisket." She set the big lidded plastic container on the counter with a thud.

"No, that I'm going to take back to Joyce. She can throw it out herself if she wants. Will you quit flouncing around? You're going to break something."

"Shelley, I don't think you're taking this seriously enough. If he can think *I* might have done it when I brought my salad, he's only half a step away from suspecting *you* of doing it a few minutes later. In fact, he might decide we were in on it together, or that one of us is covering for the other, and that way we'd *both* be in trouble. Accessory to murder is a prison term too. Oh, God—!"

The big bowl of potato salad slipped from her grip and hit the floor. The plate that had served as a lid bounced against the table leg and shattered; the bowl rolled sideways, flinging potato salad around the room.

"Oh, hell! How am I going to find a matching plate?" Shelley moaned, staring down at the mess. "Is the bowl broken?"

"No. And don't worry about the plate. It was my fault. Here." She handed Shelley the bowl and started scooping up globs of potato salad with a spatula and flinging them into the sink. "Give me a paper towel to get this glass."

Murder was forgotten while they cleaned up and

disposed of the rest of the food. Shelley washed the dishes and Jane behaved herself while she dried them and stacked them up.

"Let's go ahead and take them back," Shelley said. "If we don't, everybody will come here and talk to me endlessly about the whole thing. I'm sick of it."

"You better not get too sick of it, not with that man suspecting us."

Shelley just rolled her eyes at this. "Take Mary Ellen's bowl back while I put the rest of them in the car."

Tucking the heavy, slippery bowl firmly under her arm, Jane went across the street and rang Mary Ellen's doorbell. She answered it a moment later. Today she was in a charcoal jogging suit that set off the blond in her hair beautifully. Didn't she ever look bad?

"Jane, come in."

Jane walked through to the kitchen and set the bowl down carefully. "I'm sorry, the plate on top got broken. It was my fault. I'll get you a new one."

Mary Ellen smiled. "You can't. And I don't want you to. It was just a grocery-store giveaway. You know, you buy ten dollars' worth of stuff and get the plate for a quarter. I'm glad to see the end of it. Sit down, will you?"

"Thanks, but I can't. Shelley and I are taking all the dishes back."

"What's happening, Jane? I saw that man in the red car over there a while ago. Do they know who did it yet? I haven't seen anything more in the paper about it, and I didn't like to bother Shelley by asking questions. I know she must be awfully upset."

"They don't seem to know much," Jane said. She wasn't sure whether the theory of it being the wrong victim was supposed to be a secret or not. Probably not, or VanDyne wouldn't have told her, but still . . . "Did he come talk to you?"

"The detective? Yes. He seemed to expect to find that I spent the whole day with my nose glued to the front window, spying on the neighbors. He was disappointed, I think, at how little I knew about everybody's comings and goings."

"You didn't see anything or anybody unusual that day?"

"No. I work in the den all day, and that window faces the side yard. Unless I'm passing through the living room to do laundry or something, I never see what's going on in the street."

Jane started back toward the front door. "How's your arm?"

"Feeling better. The doctor gave me some stuff for pain, and I'm getting used to it and don't bash it into the furniture so often now."

"Do you need me to take you to the store or anything?"

"It's nice of you to offer, but Ed's been real good about helping out. He's even been cooking." She wrinkled her nose, indicating wordlessly that the intent might be noble but the results questionable.

"How long do you have to keep the cast on?"

Mary Ellen looked surprised. "I have no idea. I didn't even think to ask."

There was a *beep* in front. Shelley was honking for Jane to get a move on. "Gotta run, Mary Ellen. I'm really sorry about the plate. Are you sure—"

"Positive."

As Jane climbed into the minivan, they saw Suzie Williams come up the street and pull into her driveway. "What's she doing home?"

Jane glanced at her watch. It was only five before eleven. "Maybe an early lunch hour. Let's find out. We can get rid of one more dish."

Suzie came to the door scowling, but brightened when she saw them. "Let me guess! You're the committee for public decency, come to straighten me out."

"You probably need it," Jane said. "What are you doing home at this time of day?"

Suzie motioned them in and headed for the kitchen with Jane and Shelley in her wake. "I'm taking the rest of the day off. Cramps. I'm so sick of this filthy female plumbing. Cramps, at my age! It's all so goddamn useless. I mean, what the hell good is a uterus anyway when you're through having kids? Ovaries are okay, but a womb? It's just a damn nuisance. If hysterectomies weren't so expensive, I'd buy myself one. Coffee? Coke?"

"You're not that old," Shelley said.

"I'll be thirty-eight next month, kiddo, and if I got pregnant now, I'd shoot some guy in the balls and then put the gun in my mouth. Jesus God, have you forgotten how miserable babies are? Remember sterilizers, diapers, colic, unexplained fevers in the middle of the night that scare the shit out of you and disappear by the time the doctor's on the case?"

Suzie and Shelley chatted for a few minutes of the almost forgotten horrors—and joys—of babies. Jane was quiet, trying to observe Suzie and her house as if she were a stranger. She'd known Suzie for years and liked her outspoken, vulgar way of expressing herself and the energy she brought to anything she did or talked about. But what did she *really* know about her?

She glanced around the kitchen, looking for clues to the secret Suzie. She had nice enough things, selected with taste, but all a bit old and worn. The ornaments on the shelf over the tiny kitchen desk were all obviously school projects of Bob's. Some pictures he'd drawn, a lopsided ceramic sugar bowl, nothing that really said anything about Suzie herself. Jane couldn't remember seeing any family pictures, just school pictures of the boy displayed with pride.

Suzie rarely mentioned her ex-husband, and when she did it was in scathing terms. Jane seemed to recall that he'd left her for another woman—"A thin little bitch," as buxom Suzie put it. It was apparently some time ago, because Suzie had lived in the neighborhood since her son was in preschool. There must have been a decent divorce settlement for Suzie to have bought the house and furnished it nicely, but probably not much alimony; she made it clear that she wasn't working to 'fulfill' herself, but to keep their roof over their heads. And the furniture and carpets, while clean and neat, were beginning to show age. Bob didn't spend summers with his father like so many of the kids of divorced parents in the neighborhood, so there must not be any contact with him.

Jane searched her memory. Where was Suzie from?

Somewhere in the South, she thought. For her first few years here she'd carried on hideously about the winters. "I never thought I'd see the day when I'd go trudging around ass-deep in the snow!" she said the first time they'd met. So why *had* she come here?

"I'm asking you for the last time what you want to drink!" Suzie said, shaking Jane's arm.

"Oh! Sorry. A Coke, I think. Wasn't that one of the choices?"

"Sure, but it's full of sugar and caffeine. Do you care?"

"I wouldn't want it any other way," Jane said fervently.

"A woman after my own heart. I don't know why caffeine's suddenly got such a bad rep. First they take away our Dexedrine, then they go after caffeine. It's not fair. How's a girl to get through the day?"

"Suzie, where are you from?" Jane asked.

"Texas, why?"

"I just wondered. You don't have an accent."

"Southern accents don't take on Swedes, didn't you know? Try to picture Mrs. Olson saying 'Haf sum coffee— y'awl.' I can do it if I need to." She drew herself up, tossed her long, platinum hair, and assumed a sleepy, southern- belle look. "Ah doan know what y'awl city folks mean 'bout accents. I tawk just 'bout like my daddy. Sheeeet. It's a three-syllable word in the South, shit. She-eee-it."

Shelley choked on her drink.

"Where are you from, Jane?" Suzie asked, politely ignoring Shelley.

"Everywhere. My father was a civil servant with a genius for languages. He was also very handsome and had a good family background. So everytime anybody needed a highly presentable translator, he was it. We lived almost anywhere there had ever been an embassy. What about your folks?"

"No idea," she said breezily. "They dropped me off at an orphanage when I was two. I was raised in foster homes."

"Oh, I'm sorry."

Suzie sat down and leaned her arms on the table. "Why? It wasn't your fault, and it wasn't so bad. Foster parents have gotten a bad rep too. Most of mine were nice."

Jane had the feeling she'd said something very tactless, but couldn't tell quite what it was. Suzie and Shelley were both sipping their drinks and staring at her, as if eager to see which foot she'd put in her mouth next.

"Suzie, was Edith blackmailing you?"

Shelley gasped.

Suzie just stared at her for an extraordinarily long moment, then chuckled. "That's so goddamn unsubtle I can't believe you said it! Like something out of Monty Python. Jane, you're priceless."

"Well, was she?"

"Hell, no! What for? No, wait—let me see if I can figure this out. You think I'm a Libyan spy in disguise, this is a blond wig, and I asked the cleaning lady to dust a basement full of bombs!" She shrieked with delight. "Or maybe I'm a mass murderer who slaughtered an entire Texas town and came here to hide out. Edith found my shotgun with forty-seven notches on the handle."

Even though she was the butt of the joke, Jane found herself joining Suzie's infectious laughter. "Actually, I had you pegged for hijacking a truckload of pomegranates—"

"And Edith found her with juice running down her chin and her bra stuffed with seeds," Shelley put in.

They tossed off progressively sillier ideas for a few minutes, and Suzie finally said, "Bless your sneaky little heart, Jane, you've made me almost forget my cramps. Will you both stay for lunch? It's getting to be that time."

Shelley stood up, wiping her eyes. "Thanks, no, Suzie. I want to get as many of these dishes back as I can."

Suzie walked them to the door, still giggling. But as they started to walk away, she grew serious. "Jane, do you really think that's what the murder was about? Edith blackmailing someone? Is that what your cocky, handsome detective thinks?"

"Who knows what he thinks? He interviewed you, I hear."

"Yes, but he didn't get anywhere," she said with a lecherous look. "I didn't reveal any neighborhood secrets."

"Do you really know any?"

"Sure, so do you, if you stop and think about it. Quiet little abortions before it was legal, affairs, questionable incomes, that sort of thing. But if we know them, they're not exactly secrets anyway. But Jane, there's something you ought to think about while you're on this little private quest for the truth—"

"What?"

"Nobody's ever had the balls to try a thing like blackmail on me. Partly because I don't have anything nasty enough for it to work. But if it had been true—if she had been blackmailing me and you'd asked me—Jane, I'd have said exactly the same thing to you as I did."

Chapter Sixteen

"Who do you think you are—Miss Marple?" Shelley demanded when they got back in the car. She was obviously torn between anger and amusement.

"Well, somebody has to get to the bottom of this, and I don't have much faith in our friend Detective VanDyne, do you?"

"It *is* his job, you know."

"I know that, and he's probably pretty good at it, but this has to do with private things. Do you think anybody's going to tell him—a man, a cop, an outsider—what they were being blackmailed about?"

Shelley fished her keys out of her purse, started the engine, and backed out of Suzie's driveway at a much higher speed than was usual for her. "Probably not. No more than they're going to tell you."

"Yes, they will."

Shelley stopped at the corner and looked at her for a long moment before driving on. "Like Suzie did, huh?"

"I'll admit I struck out on that one. But I've learned a valuable lesson, and I never for a moment suspected Suzie anyway. It was a sort of trial run, you see."

"Oh, sure. If you don't suspect her, who do you suspect?"

"Actually, I think it may have been Robbie Jones." She glanced at Shelley. "You do too, don't you?"

Shelley cleared her face of the slight smile that had been starting at the corners of her mouth. "That's not fair of either of us, Jane. She's just homely and dull.

That's no reason to suspect her of murder, for God's sake."

"Shelley, if anybody's going to be suspected, it might as well be her—and I'm not going by her looks. The fact is, she's more the type than any of us. She's a superb organizer. A cold-blooded organizer, you might say. And murdering that cleaning lady took a cool head and good planning. Also, I keep thinking of that time we were having some kind of meeting and somebody mentioned how odd it was that her daughter didn't have her beautiful red hair. Remember?"

"Vaguely. She said something about her taking after her father. So what?"

"Then Suzie said she saw no resemblance to Harry, and Robbie said, no, her daughter's father was her first husband. Not the daughter's husband, Robbie's."

"Oh, yes, I remember there was a stir about that later. Nobody knew she'd been married before, and Suzie was carrying on about how she couldn't find a man to marry and Robbie had found two and it proved life wasn't fair."

"Right. But remember how Robbie clammed up after that, and nobody could get her to say another word about the first husband?"

"Yes, but none of that means a damn thing. We know lots of people who made a bad first marriage and just don't like to talk about it. Before I met Paul, I was engaged to a man once that I'd sooner die than admit I knew. I could have married him, and I certainly wouldn't want to talk about it. So what?"

"The marriage isn't what matters here, it's her secretiveness."

"Pretty thin, Jane."

"I know it is. But Shelley, think about it. What do we know about her? Almost nothing. Most of our friends have mentioned all sorts of things about their past at one time or another, but except for that one time, what has Robbie *ever* said about her life?"

"Nothing that I can remember, but when have we expressed an interest? Be honest, Jane. I've always assumed that she's always been as dull as she is now and there was nothing worth asking about or even listening to. That's our fault, not hers."

Jane lapsed into silence for a few minutes, and finally said, "I know you're right. But I still think if any of us could have done it, it would be her."

"So do I, frankly. But that isn't proof of anything."

"Shelley, you're forgetting. *We* don't need proof. We just need to figure it out and Detective VanDyne can find the proof. That's his part of the job."

"I think the whole problem is his job."

"In theory, yes. But the fact is, he doesn't seem to be in any great hurry to sort this out, and in the meantime, your kids are growing up with your sister."

"I called her last night and offered to send along the adoption papers," Shelley said. "Yes, you're right. I'm the one who wants this solved soon. It's VanDyne's job, but it's my life that's being imposed upon. So, do we go after Robbie next?"

"Might as well try. Do you suppose she's home?"

"You never know. She works a very erratic schedule at that mental hospital. I hope you've got some improved technique of questioning in mind."

"I certainly do."

Robbie did turn out to be home, but barely. "Oh, hello," she said at the door, taking her dish. "Will you come in?" She checked her watch. "I'm on my way to work, but I don't have to leave for nine minutes. Shelley, I wanted to talk to you. I'm concerned about this planning committee. We're supposed to report to the school board on our plans for the playground the end of next week, and without having had a single meeting—I know this awful death has been a great shock, but we really should be getting on with things."

"I hadn't even thought about it. You're right, of course. I'll set up another time."

"We could have the meeting here, if you'd prefer," Robbie said, but it was a halfhearted offer. Her house was one of the dozen or so scattered through the neighborhood that predated the subdivision by some twenty or thirty years. Most were big, sprawling farm homes. Others, like Robbie's, were old and small with little, oddly angled rooms. It wasn't a good place for meetings. Nor was Robbie a born hostess. Her house was uncomfortably clean, always reeking of Clorox and Lysol.

"Thanks for offering, Robbie, but I don't mind having it," Shelley said. "In a day or two I hope this terrible mess about the cleaning lady will be taken care of and I'll get back to normal."

"Oh, do they have the person who did it?"

Jane studied her for some sign of her thoughts. But that big, lantern-jawed face showed nothing but mild, impersonal interest.

"Not exactly," Shelley said, and glanced at Jane with an expression that clearly meant, "Take it away, Jane."

"You see, Robbie, it seems to have to do with blackmail," Jane said. "And what we're wondering is, what was Edith blackmailing *you* about?" She tried to make it sound as if they were all victims in this together.

Robbie's face grew suddenly pale, and Jane noticed for the first time that she had freckles. She turned her back on them, her shoulders rigid.

"Robbie, you can tell us," Jane said. Her heart was pounding; Robbie hadn't denied it. Was there about to be a shocking revelation, and did she *really* want to hear it?

"Robbie . . . ?" Shelley prodded.

She whirled back around, her skin mottled in ugly red patches. "It's none of your business!"

Shelley was the first to break the tense silence. "Robbie, I'm sorry, but it is. A perfectly innocent woman was strangled to death in my house."

"I didn't do it!"

Shelley took her hand, a clenched fist that didn't relax. "I don't imagine you did, Robbie. But I still need to know all I can find out." She was speaking very softly and soothingly. But Robbie continued to glare at her, her face stiff and hostile.

Jane was feeling sick. Was Shelley holding the very hand that had looped the vacuum cleaner cord around poor Ramona Thurgood's throat and twisted and twisted? Had they now set themselves up as the next victims? That was one aspect of this snooping that hadn't occurred to her, but now came with a force that left her nearly breathless.

"I'm not talking to you any more about this. Get out!" Robbie's command was icy.

"Yes, of course," Shelley said. She'd paled a bit too, and Jane suspected Shelley's thoughts mirrored her own: In their enthusiasm to solve the mystery, what had they stupidly unleashed?

They went to the door, scuttling sideways like frightened crabs, half-afraid to turn their backs on her.

"Get out! Get out!" she screamed as they slipped through the front door and out into the cool air.

They all but ran to the car. Shelley's hands were shaking so badly she could hardly get the key in the ignition. Neither said a word until they were back in Shelley's driveway. "Come to my house," Jane said.

They went in. There was no sign of Willard until he recognized their voices and came slinking in from the dining room cravenly wagging his tail. *Some watchdog!* Jane thought. Shelley sat down at the kitchen table and put the heels of her hands to her eyes.

"Jane, we just did something terrible."

"I know," Jane said, surprised to find that her voice was trembling.

"If Robbie Jones didn't kill Ramona, we've insulted and embarrassed a friend, probably beyond repair. If she *did*, it's worse. We've alerted her that we're on to her and—oh, God, Jane! What have we done?"

The phone rang and Jane jumped. Unable to ignore a ringing phone, no matter what the reason, she reluctantly picked it up.

"Janey, I've been calling you all morning. I was getting worried about you."

"Uncle Jim! I was out—uh, running errands with Shelley." Dear God, she couldn't tell him what they'd actually been up to. It was precisely what he had warned her against, endangering herself by knowing too much. Now she understood what he'd meant.

"I talked to a man at your local department. Nice young man. Wasn't too forthcoming, of course. Detective VanDyne was out, but I did get a little information. It seems they do feel the attack was intended against the other cleaning woman. And blackmail is the supposed motive, just as you thought. There's nothing official in her record, but she's been let go from two other agencies over some questionable practices."

"Do they know who was being blackmailed?" Jane asked.

There was a long pause. "Now, Janey, you know I can't be sharing other people's private business with you..." He paused again and went on very slowly and deliberately. "But I could point out certain things that are a matter of public record."

"Like what?"

"Well, for instance, there are newspaper accounts of an incident in a small town in upstate New York that tell about the trial, and subsequent imprisonment, of a psychiatrist who molested and seriously injured a child who was a patient of his, about ten years ago. The newspaper says that his wife—a nurse—was indicted as an accessory to the murder."

"Oh, my God!"

"This wife was later proved to have been visiting a friend in Florida at the time, and no charges were brought against her. In fact, the judge is reported to have made particular mention of her innocence, and the fact that she was an auxiliary victim. I think, if I were such a woman, I would probably change my last name and move away, wouldn't you?"

Jane cleared her throat and glanced at Shelley, who was watching her with the same morbid fascination as Max and Meow showed when watching Todd's hamsters. "What was this wife's name, Uncle Jim?"

"At that time—Roberta Cheney. You do understand this, don't you, Janey?"

"I think so. This woman was clearly innocent, but if she were still working as a psychiatric nurse, the mere association might seriously damage her career. Or she might be afraid it would."

"That's fair to say. And Jane—I would suggest that if I knew a person such as this, I would stay clear of her for the time being."

"Oh, I would too, Uncle Jim," Jane said with a sincerity that rang as false as a tin dime.

"Janey, you are minding your own beeswax, aren't you?"

"Absolutely!"

Shelley groaned.

Chapter Seventeen

Jane hung up and said, "Roberta was married to a psychiatrist who molested a patient, a child."

"Oh, no," Shelley said. "How long ago?"

"Ten years or so. Uncle Jim said that early in the investigation Robbie was considered an accessory, but was completely cleared because—" Jane stopped, listening. A car door slammed in one of their driveways. Nervous, they sat there, frozen like fugitives, until there was a light tap at Jane's kitchen door.

Jane peered through the curtains, then opened the door to Joyce Greenway. Her red convertible was parked in Shelley's driveway.

"Is Shelley here? Oh, hi, Shelley. I just stopped by to see if I could pick up that thing I brought the brisket in last week. I'm taking treats to the grade school this afternoon and I don't have anything else big enough to serve—Shelley, what's wrong? You look like a ghost."

Jane admired the way Shelley covered her built-up anxiety. "I just realized I put the brisket in the car to bring to you two hours ago. I completely forgot. If it wasn't nasty before, it probably is now. I'm so sorry!"

"Don't be. Nobody in my family will eat it anyway. Have you ever heard of anything so stupid? Say, before I forget, I wanted to ask you about that costuming book—"

Joyce was directing the local community theater production of *The Importance of Being Earnest*, and Shelley had agreed to help with the costumes. The two women fell into a discussion of patterns, giving Jane time to observe them and think quietly.

This intrusion of normal, everyday concerns calmed her, and she considered Robbie's motive for killing the cleaning lady. Driven by the need to protect her job and her daughter from the taint of her first husband's public disgrace, she'd taken the ultimate step to keep it quiet. As horrible as the thought was, Jane felt a grudging sympathy for her.

But for all that, could Jane automatically eliminate everyone else who was under suspicion? She thought not. If one woman had an adequate motive, it didn't necessarily mean others didn't. What about Joyce? A woman who dusted her luggage weekly, yet kept a cleaning lady who wasn't very good? If blackmail wasn't the reason for keeping Edith on, what was? Certainly not her charming personality.

Jane propped her feet up on the vacant chair and leaned back, nursing her coffee along and studying Joyce with a trace of jealousy. She was simply adorable, there was no other word for it. Her fine, blond hair was fashionably kinky and fluffy and set off her fragile features—enormous blue eyes, a mouth that just missed being an old-fashioned Cupid's bow. And the figure that went with this was perfect. Generous breasts and shapely hips on a slim, girlish frame.

She looked—dammit!—about twenty-five. Jane knew they had to be the same age. Joyce might even be older than she. How dare she look so good? Of course, her husband was a plastic surgeon, and she'd probably had her full quota of eye lifts, tummy tucks, breast enlargements and whatever other miracles they could work these days.

What could a woman like this need to hide? Something to her husband's detriment, perhaps? Jane had doctor husbands on the brain. Would Joyce kill somebody to protect her husband? She seldom mentioned him. He seemed to be a workaholic, while Joyce was a 'social-holic.' Jane couldn't remember ever seeing them together. One or the other of them was always at soccer games and back-to-school nights—usually Joyce—but never both. Jane had never even seen him in the audience at the community theater productions. If there was a tremendous passion or loyalty in that marriage, it wasn't evident.

Aside from a possible motive, and probably more important, could she have done it? Was it physically possible? Strangling somebody must take a lot of strength. Certainly the victim fought back. Even Jane could probably toss tiny Joyce around like kindling if she tried. But, as she considered this, an image flashed through her mind. She'd gone with Shelley to a rehearsal one night last spring, and Joyce had been there, carting stage scenery around with the abandon of a seasoned dockhand. And then, if you add the sheer adrenaline of fear . . .

Joyce had gotten sidetracked from theater concerns momentarily and was telling a Polish joke. "—and the other one said, 'I know why we didn't get any ducks. We weren't throwing the dogs high enough.' "

Jane had heard it before and laughed politely. Shelley hadn't, and her laugh was a bit giddy, just short of going out of control.

Get your thoughts organized, Jane scolded herself. Supposing Joyce *could* have done it, why *would* she? Asking 'Are you being blackmailed?' didn't work, as her conversation with Suzie had proved. She had to figure this out fast; Joyce was looking for her car keys.

"I've got to run," she said, standing. "Edith is off sick today and I have a substitute. I want to keep an eye on what she's doing. . . ."

Did she mean how well she was cleaning, or was there a concealed worry that this one would snoop around and find out something too?

"Joyce, wait a sec. There's something I want to talk to you about."

"I don't think this is the time—" Shelley said, shaking her head in warning. "Don't you have to pick Todd up from school?"

"I don't drive this afternoon," Jane said. "Joyce, I think there's something I should tell you. I know why Edith is blackmailing you."

Joyce's eyes opened even wider, and she sat back down with a thump. "Oh . . ."

Ah-hah, it's true, then, Jane thought.

Joyce's tiny chin was trembling, just like a child

trying not to cry. "Oh, Jane. I didn't want anybody to know. Ever."

How am I going to get her to tell what it was while acting like I already know? I should have worked this out better, Jane thought in a panic. She kept her voice calm. "We're your friends. You can talk about it to us."

Now the tears came. "You're a saint, Jane. Have you known all this time and never said anything?"

Jane nodded sympathetically. Joyce took out a tissue and blew her nose. Shelley looked across the table at Jane, her eyes wild with questions. Jane sketched a tiny shrug. Shelley rolled her eyes and suppressed a groan.

"I've been living in absolute terror all these months that you'd find out somehow." Joyce blew her nose again. Her pretty face was streaked with tears, and her mascara was running. "That terrible Edith came on the wrong day the second time I had her and caught us, otherwise nobody would have ever known . . ."

Us? Caught doing what?

"It's all right," Shelley said soothingly.

"All right? Oh, no. Of course it's not. It was horrible. I can see that now. It would have been the worst mistake anybody ever made. Stupid and cruel. I've come to hate myself for even thinking of it."

What was *she talking about? Planning a bank robbery? Did Edith find the gang sitting around the living room with floor plans and blueprints?*

Joyce reached out and took Jane's hand. "I can't imagine why you didn't just kill me. I thought at first you knew, and then when you didn't say anything, I started thinking that maybe you didn't. I never knew just what happened, you see—"

Jane's fingers tensed.

"—and the newspaper reports didn't say which way the vehicles were headed when it happened, and I thought maybe he hadn't even been home yet to tell you—"

A lump the size of a frozen basketball was forming in Jane's stomach.

"—and I couldn't really ask, could I? Jane, it was all my fault. Really, it was. It was just a fling in his eyes. At least at first. He'd have come back to you. I'm certain of it.

My life would have been ruined, but it would have been just what I deserved. Actually, in an awful way, I didn't mind paying the blackmail. It was the only way I could pay for my sin—"

Jane pulled her hand away slowly and got up. Looking as stricken as Jane felt, Shelley was on her feet instantly, but Jane put out her hand in a mute gesture to hold her off. "Oh, Jane!" she said, her voice breaking. "I'm so sorry!"

Joyce looked from Jane to Shelley and back again. Comprehension began to dawn. "What—what is happening? Oh, God! You didn't know!" She put her head on the table and began to sob. "My g-g-goddamn big m-m-mouth! Now I've m-m-made it worse!"

Picking up her purse, Jane went to the door to the garage like a sleepwalker.

"Wait, I'll come with you!" Shelley cried.

"No! Thank you, but I'd rather just have a little time to myself," Jane said. Part of her recognized and complimented herself on how calm and well behaved she was being.

She pulled up the garage door, got in the car, buckled her seat belt, checked the rearview mirror, and backed out carefully. She drove away, leaving Joyce Greenway crying at her kitchen table.

Chapter Eighteen

The shopping center was two miles from Jane's house. When she and Steve had first moved into their home, the spot was an open field. A few years later the land had been cleared, graded, and "improved" by the building of a gigantic complex of shops, restaurants, and movie theaters. Adjacent property had been purchased for possible expansion, but had never been put to use. The shopping center parking lot, far larger than needed, still backed up to what had once been a Christmas tree farm.

It was here that Jane and Steve had come years ago on a frigid, windy Sunday with Mike and Katie, both of them dressed in quilted snowsuits that made them look like brightly colored Pillsbury Doughboys. They had carefully dug up a small fir tree that sat in the living room in a bucket for the holidays and then went outdoors. It now shaded the patio from the afternoon sun. It, like the children, had grown beyond recognition.

The trees on the farm had been neglected. Those nearest the parking lot had grown brown and dingy from traffic fumes. Many had died, others were stunted and twisted. A stand near the north end had been wiped out by a fire started by lightning the previous spring. Scattered stumps showed where a few had been cut. But those remaining were towering now, and made dark, secret places. Today, the abandoned Christmas tree farm looked as desolate as Jane felt.

She stopped the car at the very end of the shopping center lot. There was nothing near her but cracked asphalt, crumbling curbing, and a rusted lamp standard that

someone had backed into and bent. They didn't even paint
parking lines this far from the shops. She turned off the engine and stared at the trees, trying to recapture the simple
and happy life of that December day, when the children
were little and she didn't suspect that Steve would ever
stop loving her.

Damn him to hell!

She let herself topple over sideways, her face resting
on the upholstery fabric. Tears boiled over, and she
wrapped her arms around her head, sobbing. For a long
time she had no thoughts, no words, just a heart-
constricting agony fighting to get out. She cried until
she was exhausted.

It had all happened so long ago. She was well along
the road of getting over it. Or had been, until a few
minutes ago. Why should this information have been so
devastating?

Because she'd always assumed it was someone from
work: some cute sales rep from one of the drug firms—
they were using a lot more women these days—or a
customer, or a beautiful young pharmaceutical graduate.
Somebody safe and anonymous. She'd never even dreamed
the woman he'd left her for was someone she knew. A
friend! Well, not much of a friend, as it appeared
now.

All this time it had been Joyce Greenway. A woman
like herself. Like herself. That was the painful part, not
even the fact that they knew each other.

That frosting job of Joyce's certainly concealed the
same occasional gray hairs Jane had. The tummy tucks
couldn't erase stretch marks. Dammit! Joyce's hormones
were running down at a rate equal to everybody else's.
Joyce drove the same teenage children in car pools, she
had the same cleaning lady, the same civic committees and
concerns, the same orthodontist for the kids. The times
they'd sat around that waiting room together while braces
were being tightened!

It hadn't hurt as much before—not that Jane had
known there were degrees of pain in such a rejection—
thinking she'd lost him to someone young and free-spirited.
Male menopause, Shelley called it. The mad, male urge to

prove fading virility with a young woman when his wife was showing her years, and so was he. That wasn't fair, but it was vaguely understandable. Jane had pictured the woman as different from her in every possible way. Young, firm-bodied, with no repressions whatsoever. No responsibilities beyond pleasure. She'd told herself, *No wonder I lost him to someone like that. I couldn't compete with youth.*

But Joyce—!

Why Joyce? What in the world did she have to offer that Jane didn't? Aside from a better figure, prettier hair, a softer voice, a more expensive wardrobe?

And why hadn't she suspected? Of course, Joyce was a fine actress. She'd been trained to convincingly present another persona on the stage, and could apparently use that skill off the stage as well. Naturally she'd been able to conceal her feelings. Acting the neutral, nonsexual, nonthreatening neighbor at block parties and PTA functions. Had she and Steve sneaked off for a quick grope behind the cotton candy machine at the junior high carnival? Had their hands touched while turning hamburgers on the grill? Had they exchanged sultry looks across the small desks on back-to-school nights at the grade school? That time he went to help her with a flat tire—had he been fumbling around with her blouse buttons instead of the car jack?

She heard a car engine approaching and sat up, furiously wiping her eyes.

The minivan cast a shadow Jane recognized. Shelley opened the passenger door of Jane's station wagon. "May I come in?"

"If you don't mind being seen with a woman whose mascara is all over her chin."

"You aren't wearing mascara. You can't fool me." She got in and closed the door. "For whatever it's worth, Joyce looks worse than you do. Here." Shelley had unearthed a travel pack of tissues from her purse and handed them to Jane. "Mop up, honey. Got any car pools you want me to pick up this afternoon? It's almost that time."

"No, thanks, I'm off today. Did you get her out of my house?"

"Yes. She actually got so hysterical I had to slap her. Just like in the movies. I've always wanted to do that, but I never thought I'd enjoy it so much."

Jane smiled weakly. "I wish I'd had the chance. Shelley, the truth—did you know before?"

Shelley hitched herself around sideways and looked at Jane with a horrified expression. "Good God! No, of course not. Do you think I would have let that happen to you? I'd have hated telling you, but I'd have done it. Even if I only suspected."

"How did you find me here?"

"I just guessed."

"You did not. You're a terrible liar."

"No, I knew you came here a lot last winter. I saw your car a couple of times when I came to the shopping center."

"This was a Christmas tree farm. That fir by my patio came from here. Why would he want her? Her?"

"I can't imagine and neither should you. It was insanity."

"Male menopause. But why somebody just as old and busy and ordinary as me? I thought it was some nubile young thing who wore crotchless panties every day and still had her breasts up under her chin, where ours started out."

"Madness, Jane. You can't explain it. Nobody can."

"Now that I think about it, I wonder why *she* considered it. Steve wasn't such a noticeable treasure. He wasn't any better-looking than her husband, and he certainly didn't have as much money. I have the feeling the Greenways are rolling in it."

"Maybe she just wanted the attention," Shelley said. "You know her husband never has time for anything with her or the family. Steve was good about that."

Jane tilted her head back so the tears wouldn't run down her face. "He was. That he was."

After a long moment, Shelley said, "You got her off the hook with Edith, you know. That's why she was blackmailing her—threatening to tell you about her and Steve. You've done the bitch a favor."

Jane started chuckling, then laughing. Shelley joined her. Finally, when they'd both calmed down a bit, Shelley said, "I don't suppose she'd have killed the woman to keep it from you."

Jane looked perplexed. "That *was* how it started, wasn't it? I'd completely forgotten about the murder. I don't suppose she would have killed Edith. But, Shelley, I don't care anymore. You were right when you said it was the job of the police to figure it out. I'm not doing any more snooping. God only knows what else I might find out!"

"Couldn't be anything much worse. Not that I'm encouraging you to pry into any more secrets. The next one might be something that would drive *me* to this parking lot. Jane, there is something you need to think about, though. How are you going to resolve this?"

"With Joyce? What's to resolve? It's over. Steve's dead and neither of us have him. God! No wonder she's been so damned sweet and concerned about how I'm getting along without him! It was sheer guilty conscience. And remember what a mess she was at his funeral?"

"Yes, we talked about it. How she was a better friend of yours than we knew—to be so upset on your behalf. It wasn't you she was sorry for. It was herself!"

"Do you suppose her husband suspects?"

"Probably not. He might not care if he did. For what comfort it might be, that must have crossed her mind as well. But, Jane, to get back to what I was trying to say. You've got to think out what your attitude toward her is going to be."

"I don't understand."

"Well, if you're going to make a point of hating her in a public way—which I wouldn't blame you for—people are going to wonder why."

"So what? I don't care if they know she's a husband-stealing slut."

"I'm not so sure. It's fine to make her look as bad as she is, but think what it'll make you look like."

Jane stared at the ragged Christmas trees. A crow had landed on the top of one and was swaying back and forth drunkenly. "Do you have any cigarettes along?"

"I brought yours. Here."

Jane lit a cigarette, coughed, and rolled down the

car window to throw it out. "That tastes awful. I see what you mean about Joyce. She'd look like trash, which she is, but I'd look pitiful, like just what I am—a woman who couldn't keep her husband's interest and lost him to a neighbor."

"Right. It's sort of noble and tragic and romantic to be a widow. At least no one blames you for it or thinks less of you. But a deserted wife? You know how people are. They'd start wondering what Joyce had that you didn't."

"That's what I'm wondering too."

"Oh, Jane! Don't say that. You need to start getting out in the world a bit more. Meeting men who can reassure you of all your good qualities that Steve had gotten too familiar with to appreciate."

Jane scrubbed at her damp face with the crumpled tissue. "That's nice of you to say. But—" She glanced at her watch. "Where I need to get now is home. The kids'll be there in a few minutes and they'll wonder where I am. I like to be home when they get there."

"What are you going to do about Joyce?"

"Nothing. Yet. I'm just going to avoid her and let her stew in her own juices while I make up my mind."

"That's the way, Jane. You know, right now, I think she's even more miserable than you are."

"I hope so. God, I *hope* so!"

"Want me to drive you home?"

"Thanks. I'm fine now. No, I'm no such thing. But I can drive. I want to clean up my face before the kids see me. I don't want them to think anything is wrong."

Shelley took her hand, patted it, then got out of the car and stood waving as she drove away.

Jane hurried home, feeling a little better. Not happier, but somehow purged. She parked and dashed into the house. The phone was ringing, but she ignored it and ran upstairs. She flung her purse toward the bed as she dashed into the bathroom. She washed her face in warm water, then sponged her red eyes with cold. Carefully, she put on fresh make-up and combed her hair. Studying herself in the mirror, she said, "Not too bad."

She went back into the bedroom and picked up her purse. An object in the middle of the bed caught her eye.

A piece of paper with something on top. She stepped around the side of the bed to reach for it, then drew her hand back with a cry.

The note said, "MIND YOUR OWN BUSINESS."

The new paring knife was driven through the paper and into the mattress.

Chapter Nineteen

Jane opened her lingerie drawer and threw an armload of underwear over the paring knife and note so that the children wouldn't see it if they came in. It would look like she'd been sorting laundry. Then she closed the bedroom door.

They'd be here any minute. Panic rose in her throat like a bubble. After taking a few long breaths, she dialed Shelley's number, but it rang six times without an answer. Jane hung up when Katie came to the door.

"What are you doing with your door shut, Mom?"

"Oh, was it shut?" Jane said, forcing a smile that made her lips hurt.

"Mom, you're acting weird. Jenny's mom is waiting. If it's okay with you, she said Jenny and I could go with her to watch her get her hair frosted. Okay? I'll be back in time for dinner, and I don't have any homework. How do you think I'd look with my hair frosted?"

Jane reached for her purse and took out a twenty-dollar bill. "Here, why don't you treat Jenny and her mom to dinner at the mall?"

"Huh?" Katie stared at the money as if it might bite. "You're giving me this and I didn't even ask?"

"Yes, now go. Go."

"Oh-*kay*!"

Jane closed the bedroom door again and followed Katie downstairs. Mike was just coming in. He dumped his backpack full of books on top of Katie's on the kitchen floor. "Listen, Mom, a bunch of the guys asked me to play a little basketball and go for pizza. Do you care?"

"No, that's fine."

He had his mouth open, ready to launch into an argument on behalf of his plans. "Hey, you sick or something? You look kinda pale."

"Just tired," she said.

"Hey, in band this morning, old Bellhaven started having a big fit 'cause nobody was marching in time, so he makes us go in the band room and sits us all down. He's hopping around and yelling his head off like he does, and he goes up to the board and writes these huge letters *P—R—I—D—E*, see? And he says, 'I want you all to have some of this!' And he bangs his fist on the board. Old Scott's sitting back there, tapping away with the sticks and so he stands up and says, 'Thanks, Mr. Bellhaven, I'll take the *D.*'"

Jane forced a smile.

"Mom, what's wrong? You usually like Scott stories."

She wanted to hug him and assure him that she loved Scott stories and loved him more and wouldn't let anything happen to him. But instead she punched him on the arm and said, "Couldn't sleep last night, that's all. Tell me again tomorrow when I'm awake and I'll laugh. I promise. Now get along to your basketball game."

Unlike Joyce Greenway, she was a rotten actress. Mike headed for the door, then paused. "Are you really sure it's okay if I go?"

"Positive."

Two down, one remaining.

Shelley drove up as Mike was leaving on his bike. Jane ran out to meet her. She could see the woman who drove Todd's car pool on Mondays coming down the street. "Shelley, go up to my bedroom and carefully lift the underwear off the bed. I've got to get rid of Todd. I don't want the kids to know."

Shelley got out of the minivan. "Don't want them to know what?"

"You'll see. Don't touch anything but the underwear."

Shelley went inside. Jane waited for the gray Volkswagen to pull in the drive. Todd tumbled out, wrestling with Elliot Wallenberg. "Mom, can Elliot stay here and play soldiers?"

"Honey, I've got a headache. Why don't you both go play soldiers at Elliot's instead?"

That was agreeable to them and, giggling, they piled back into the car. Fortunately, the Monday driver was a woman Jane hardly knew, a brand-new addition to the neighborhood, and she was spared having to make pleasant conversation. By the time Jane got back to the house, Shelley was standing at the door. She had one hand over her mouth as if physically stopping a scream.

"Have you called the police?"

Jane came inside and watched out the window to make sure the gray Rabbit hadn't turned back for any reason. "Not yet. I didn't want the kids to know. I'll call now. Do you have that number for Detective VanDyne? I don't know what I've done with it."

"I've got it at home. Wait, isn't that it on the pad next to the phone?"

"Yes. I wonder if whoever did this noticed that I keep his number handy for constant communication?" She dialed. "Detective VanDyne, this is Jane Jeffry. I need you to come right over. Someone has stabbed my bed. I mean, well—come over and you'll see what I mean. No, wait! No sirens. Please don't come with sirens or police cars."

She hung up before he could ask her any questions, then went into the living room and flung herself down on the sofa, staring at the ceiling. Shelley plopped down in a most unShelleylike manner in the chair across from her.

"If I kept a diary, I could have a whole month's worth for this one day. It will live in my memory forever, unfortunately."

"For heaven's sake, Jane, don't go on about diaries. Tell me about that knife in your bed!"

"There's nothing to tell you. It was there like that when I came home. I saw it and threw some clothes over it, and got to work trying to find you and get the kids safely out of the house without alarming them."

"Who put it there?"

"Shelley! That's a dumb question. All I know is it's there. Could Joyce have done it before you got her out?"

"No, she was all but clinging to me the whole time. I had to pry her fingers off my arm to get her into her car."

"Did you lock the door?"

"Jane, I've been combing my brain to remember. I just don't know. I pulled it shut. If you had the button turned, it locked. Did you?"

Jane put her arm over her eyes and sighed. "I have no idea. No idea."

The doorbell rang and Jane tried to get up. She was so emotionally exhausted that her legs wouldn't even move right. She was almost woozy, like coming out of ether in the dentist's office.

Shelley jumped up. "Stay there. I'll let him in."

Jane heard the door opening and Shelley's soft tones. Then there was the creaking of the third step as her friend took Van Dyne upstairs to see the knife and note. Absurdly, she was wishing the underwear she'd strewn around the bed was lacy stuff, not practical, white cotton.

She heard them come downstairs and go from door to door, checking the locks. Apparently the knife had changed Detective VanDyne's mind about her, because when he and Shelley came back into the living room a few minutes later, he was pleasant and polite. "I'd like to have a man from the lab over. May I use your phone?"

"Ask him to come in a plain car, not a police car," Shelley said. "Jane doesn't want her children frightened."

"Of course."

He was back in a moment. Jane managed to pull herself upright. "When did this happen?" he asked.

"I found it about three-thirty. I had been gone from about two or two-thirty."

"It wasn't there before that?"

Jane struggled to think back. "I don't remember if I was in that room anytime today after I got dressed. I don't think so."

"No hurry. Just think it out step by step. Talk it through if that helps."

"All right. I got the kids off to school and left to ride with Shelley to get birdseed around quarter of nine."

"Did you lock the house? I don't see any obvious evidence of forced entry."

"Yes, that time I locked up. I'm sure of it."

"When did you get back?"

Jane looked at Shelley and shrugged. "Around nine-thirty or ten?" Shelley nodded. Jane went on. "I came inside, and a few minutes later Shelley came over. We went over to her house, and you called."

VanDyne flipped a page of the small notebook he was writing in. "That was at 10:08. Did you lock up the house then?"

"I don't know. I think so. You came over when?"

"Twenty minutes later."

"I didn't go back home after that for a while. When you left, we cleaned up the kitchen and put all the borrowed dishes in Shelley's minivan to take back. We went to Suzie Williams's house first—"

"You drove next door?"

"We didn't mean to, exactly. But yes. She was just getting home as we were leaving. We stayed a few minutes, and then we went to see Robbie Jones."

VanDyne looked up from his note-taking, an eyebrow lifted. "You weren't, by any chance, trying to do my job for me, were you?"

"Whatever do you mean?" Jane asked, sounding even to herself like Miss America being asked if she were a virgin.

"I mean, it's odd that you happened to be visiting with the very people I'm questioning."

Jane slipped off her sneaker and started massaging her foot as if she had a sudden cramp.

Shelley said, "Jane, I think we better tell him."

"What kind of friend are you?" Jane asked. She was joking, but embarrassed. "All right. We were trying to find out if and why they were being blackmailed by that awful Edith."

"And were they?"

"Oh, yes. At least two of them were. Suzie says not and I believe her. But Robbie and Joyce—" Jane stopped. She could feel the hateful tears filling her eyes again. She wasn't going to break down and make a bleary-eyed, blubbering fool of herself in front of him. Bad enough that he now knew she wore boring white underwear.

"I don't mean to upset you. We know about Mrs. Jones. Robbie. But not about Mrs. Greenway."

Shelley sat forward, as if to speak, but Jane put up a hand to stop her. "My husband, my late husband—" She paused, taking a deep breath. "My late husband was leaving me for Joyce Greenway the night he—*became* my late husband."

There, she'd said it.

He had the good grace to look surprised. "I am sorry I had to know that, Mrs. Jeffry. Jane. Off the record, I've also got to tell you I find it hard to believe."

"Oh, it's true enough. She admitted—"

"No, what I meant was; I've interviewed you and I've interviewed her and I can't imagine—"

Jane felt herself blushing. Actually blushing. *Oh, well, he'll probably think it's a hot flash.* "Will you be able to tell anything about the person who did this from the paper the note was on? I've read that the police can trace paper—"

"It was the back of your electric bill."

"She could have at least used a brand of paper only made in Singapore between March and July of the year she was there with her brother—"

"She? Singapore? What?"

"I was just thinking about mystery books. It always turns on something like that." Now she was back on familiar ground, he was scowling at her again. It was oddly comforting. "We only talked to Suzie Williams, Robbie Jones, and Joyce Greenway. It had to be one of them."

"Or somebody they talked to about your—questioning," he said.

"You mean snooping. I guess that's true. but I'm pretty sure neither Robbie nor Joyce would have gotten right on the phone to talk to somebody else about it."

He leaned back and studied her for a long moment. She felt like a used car about to get its tires kicked. "You think you know who did this, don't you?"

"It doesn't matter what I think. I've had ample proof today of the general failure of my perceptions."

"Still, I'd like to know your opinion."

Shelley nodded her encouragement, and Jane said, "For what it's worth, I'm certain it's Robbie Jones. Suzie Williams was pretty much amused by my questions. Joyce

Greenway—well, she was as upset as I was by my know-ing. Not that I'd like to give her public credit for having a conscience, but I think she probably went home and just kept crying. But Robbie was furious. She screamed at us to get out of her house and kept on screaming. I've never seen anybody look at me with such hatred."

"And all these women were home all day?"

"No, Suzie was just coming home from work early, and Joyce doesn't have a job. Robbie said she was leaving for work in nine minutes, but that was when we got there. She might have changed her mind."

"I'll check on it." The doorbell rang. "That must be my man from the lab. I'll get it." He went to answer the door, talked for a minute with the newcomer, and sent him up the stairs.

When he came back, Jane said, "He won't be long, will he? I don't want the kids to know what danger they're in. What danger I've *put* them in."

"You didn't mean to. And, frankly, you were able to find out at least one thing that we might have never known. Now, you need to decide where you're going to go."

"Go? Why should I go anywhere? Oh, you mean in case Ro—the person who did this comes back. I see. Do I have to go? I'd have to explain it all to the kids and—"

"Don't you have some relatives you can stay with?"

"Only my mother-in-law—and I'd rather move into a kennel of rabid dogs."

"Well, I could ask the county if they can spare an officer to stay here, but they're pretty short-staffed as it is, and I don't know how long it would be."

"What about your Uncle Jim?" Shelley asked.

"He's offered, but it's so far out of his way, and if it's going to be for long—"

"I hope it won't be any time at all," VanDyne said. "But I can't make any promises."

"You mean this could just drag on forever? What are you going to do to solve it?"

"Everything we can."

The man from the lab came downstairs just then and handed VanDyne a note. He read it and said to Shelley and Jane, "Mrs. Jones came to work in a disturbed state today and left after a half hour."

He made no further comment then, but simply rose and tucked his notebook into his jacket pocket. Jane stood too, and walked to the front door with him and the lab man, who was carrying a plastic bag.

The lab man went to his car, but VanDyne paused. "Mrs. Jeffry, Mrs. Nowack—in the normal course of such an investigation, I wouldn't have told you that. But you have created an abnormal situation by conducting your own research. I *don't* need to point out the danger and tell you to stop, do I?"

"Of course not. I'm reformed. From now on I mind only my own business," Jane said fervently.

That sounded familiar. Hadn't she said the same thing to Uncle Jim just this morning? This time she meant it.

Chapter Twenty

Uncle Jim was furious. "You went around *telling* those women you knew they were being blackmailed? Oh, Jane, Jane, Jane. Your parents didn't raise a dummy! Why in the world did you do a thing like that?" His voice crackled over the telephone wire.

He'd never spoken to her that way, she'd never felt she deserved it as much as she did now.

With no attempt to defend herself, she said, "Will you come stay with us for a day or two? Just the nights, Uncle Jim. I'll feed you fantastically well to make up for the inconvenience I know I'm putting you to."

He heard the fright in her voice. "Of course I will, Janey."

He was there within the hour. She met him at the door with a whispered warning. "I haven't told the kids why you're here or anything about the threat. I don't want them to know. Shut up, Willard!" The dog, knowing the guest and sure he was no intruder, was making much of acting the fierce watchdog.

"Right. Are they here now?"

"Just Todd. He's out in the backyard, trying to make a paper airplane fly. Mike and Katie ought to be back pretty soon. They're eating out. Let me get you settled. I have a tuna casserole in the oven for us. You do like that, don't you?"

"As long as it's never been frozen in a little tray."

Once she had him installed in the tiny room that served as a sewing room and emergency guest room, he sat down on the edge of the narrow bed and she took a

chair by the window. Todd was still out back, and had
flown half a dozen sheets of notebook paper into the field
behind the house where they fluttered around like con-
fused ghosts.

"Janey, I've been thinking about what you told me.
Answer a few things for me—what about the doors? Were
any of them forced?"

"Not that anyone can tell. But the last time I left the
house, I'm not sure the kitchen door got locked. I wasn't
that last to leave. Shelley was, and we were all upset about
something else."

"Something else?"

Jane paused a moment, then launched into a full
account of her hideous conversation with Joyce Greenway.
Uncle Jim took out a pipe and accessories and made a
busy production of preparing to smoke it while she talked.
It was a little easier this time. While telling Detective
VanDyne, she'd feared seeing his contempt. But with
Uncle Jim, she dreaded his pity. As she spoke, she recog-
nized with another part of her mind that she was really
sick and tired of pity. She'd had a lifetime quota since
Steve died.

"The funny thing is, in the first month or so after he
died, I was almost obsessed with finding out who it was. It
seemed important and somehow necessary to discover.
Then I sort of lost interest. No, that wasn't it. I just
assumed it was someone I didn't know anyway, so what
was the point?"

Jim waited until she got this out of her system, then
quietly asked, "Would you think this woman would kill to
keep you from finding out about her and Steve?"

"I'd love to suspect her, but no, I don't think she
would have. The revelation won't change her life. It was
merely something she felt guilty and embarrassed about,
not threatened. She more or less admitted she was paying
the blackmail just to assuage her conscience."

"Threatened is the operative word, I think."

"What do you mean?"

"Well, the business of the knife in the bed—it's
clearly a threat."

"I'll say!"

"The point is, it could have been for real."

Jane got up and found him an ashtray. Sitting back down in the straight chair by the window, she said, "You mean it's somebody who doesn't really *want* to kill me? Just shut me up and make me stop meddling?"

"It's possible. If this woman could slip in and out of the house in the daytime when you're gone without notice, she could certainly do it at night, or when you were home, and put the knife into you instead of the mattress. What about keys? Do any of your neighbors have keys to the house?"

Jane looked down at her hands. How was she going to break this to him? Might as well just dump the whole truth in his lap. "Nearly everybody. For a while after Steve died, I was handing them out like free samples at the grocery store. Shelley went to the hardware store and got me a half dozen of them."

"Good God!"

"Uncle Jim, people were coming in and out, helping. Bringing food, taking care of the pets, staying with the kids while I was seeing funeral directors and lawyers and police. But we all have keys to each other's houses. You know, somebody has to go to a teacher conference, but gives a neighbor a key to let in the plumber or cable television people or whatever. We all do it all the time. We have to, or we'd be slaves to our houses."

It was obvious he was appalled at such a system. "Didn't any of them give them back?"

"I don't remember. Probably not. And I didn't think to ask for them. There was no reason to think it was dangerous to have keys out with my—my friends. Oh, Uncle Jim, I want more than anything to go back to the wandering-maniac theory..."

"Sure you do, but this maniac could hardly know you'd spent the day out picking your neighbors' lives apart, could he?"

She was spared answering his accusation by the sound of bounding footsteps on the stairs. "Hey, Mom," Mike yelled. "Is that Uncle Jim's car in front?"

"Right here, son."

"Hey, neat! What are you doing here?" Mike asked with a grin.

Jim got up and took the boy in an affectionate headlock that made Jane cringe. "Just camping out for a couple days. My apartment's being painted and the stink drove me out. I've got tomorrow off work too, so I thought I'd see how this driving of yours is coming along. I'll take you to school—*uughff*!"

Mike was pummelling him in the stomach in a halfhearted attempt to break his grip. "Gotcha!" he mumbled into Jim's armpit.

"Think you can beat the old man? I'll show you a thing or two, you skinny kid! You need to put some muscle on those bones."

Jane left them wrestling their way around the room and went down to check on the casserole. The sounds of scuffling followed her. Mike needed a grown man in his life, she thought. He never talked about missing his dad, but he must. Wasn't that kind of rough-and-ready male camaraderie important to a boy of his age?

She turned off the oven and suddenly remembered that she had a chair problem. The kitchen table had five chairs, but after Steve died, she'd put one of them in the basement so they weren't reminded at every meal of his absence. She had to find the missing chair. Of course, they could eat in the dining room, but that seemed too formal, and besides, tuna casserole wasn't "company" food.

Katie came in, bubbling with enthusiasm for hairfrosting. "I think it would look great on me, Mom. I'm sure it would make me look taller, and it only costs sixty dollars. If you'd give me fifty, I could—"

"Uncle Jim's visiting while his apartment's being painted," Jane interrupted. "I know you've had dinner, but I want you to sit with us anyway. You want to set the table or find the extra chair?"

Katie considered it carefully, then grinned. "What's easier?"

"It's a toss-up."

"Then I'll get the chair. It'll be neat having Uncle Jim stay here. I'm going to ask him what he thinks of frosted hair. I bet he'll agree with me."

Over dinner—which Mike ate as if he'd fasted for a week—Jim told the kids stories about their grandfather as a boy. Some of them were new to Jane, and she had a suspicion he was making them up for the sake of entertainment, but it didn't matter. Funny family stories were a perfect antidote to the distress and horror she'd felt for the last few days. Jane cleared the table and started the dishwasher. She gave Max and Meow the leftover casserole, and treated Willard to a glob of raw hamburger so he'd leave the cats alone to eat.

Jim and Todd adjourned to the living room, where the older man helped the boy with his math homework. When Jane was through in the kitchen, she was surprised to discover that Mike and Katie had both brought their books in and were working in the same room. Katie seldom got that far from the phone when she was home.

"Janey, you look beat," Uncle Jim said, looking up from the problem he and Todd were solving. "Why don't you go on to bed? The kids and I will finish here and lock up for the night."

She eagerly took him up on the offer. Upstairs, she straightened up her bedroom, then stripped the wounded bed and remade it with fresh sheets. Soon enough she'd have to figure out what to do about the hole in the mattress, but not tonight. She got out her most treasured, expensive bath oil and took a long, hot soak. She tried not to think, but it was impossible to completely clear her mind. This peaceful, domestic evening had relaxed some of her tensions, but she could feel new ones coiling.

It was awfully nice to have a man in the house again. Aside from all the frightening events that had brought him here, it was comforting to know that, for once, another responsible adult was going to make sure the kids went to bed at a decent hour, lock up the house, and make sure Willard went out one last time. Jane hadn't fully realized the burden she'd been carrying as the only adult in the family until she'd gotten this brief opportunity to lay down a few of those tasks.

She wasn't the only one who appreciated Uncle Jim's presence. The kids were obviously thrilled to have him. Sunday visits were a different matter—on Sundays he was a guest, *her* guest. Tonight he belonged here, belonged to them.

Those children need a father, a voice inside her said.

"Damn you, Steve!" she said out loud to the bathroom she'd shared with him until a few months ago. "What gave you the right to do this to us?"

And you *need a man,* the voice added slyly.

"I've had one husband. I don't want another one."

Not a husband. A man, the voice intoned patiently.

Jane closed her eyes and sank down further in the hot, scented water.

Chapter Twenty-one

It had been five days now since Ramona Thurgood had been murdered, and Jane was getting desperate for life to return to normal. Tuesday, however, promised to be outstanding as one of the most boring days of her life. Of course, anything would have paled in comparison to the events and revelations of Monday. The contrast was increased by Uncle Jim's watchful presence. He wasn't about to let her out of his protective range without good reason.

At least he, unlike the kids, appreciated the gigantic breakfast she fixed. Willard, who had his big brown eyes peeled for leftovers, was disappointed in the slim pickings. After riding along while Mike drove his car to school, Jim let Jane leave with Katie and again with Todd, apparently feeling there was minimal danger at that hour of the morning.

"I think I'd rather figure out the schedules for the New York subway system than try to unravel your itinerary," he said when she returned from the last morning run.

"It's not so bad when you get used to it. Todd's in a car pool with five kids and five drivers, so each of us does both back and forth one day a week. Every Tuesday all year is mine. Mike's in with three band members, so I drive his every third week, except today was someone else's turn I had to take and we'll make it up next time it's my week—"

"You'll all remember this driving debt?"

"You bet. It's like a Mafia vendetta. Now, Katie's car

155

pools this year are a little more complicated. She's in with
four girls, but two of them are sisters, so I drive three
mornings a week, another mother drives three afternoons
and the mother of the two drives morning and afternoon
on Thursdays and Fridays. Of course, while cheerleading
practice is going on the first month, I drive her myself and
the other two mothers share equally, except when—"

"Stop! It's as bad as I thought. Worse! Now, is there
anything you need done around here? I might as well be
useful."

"Good Lord, it's good enough of you to come. I can't
put you to work besides." She paused. "I do wonder,
however, about the furnace. Do you know anything about
furnaces? I have a man coming Friday, but—"

He disappeared to the basement with a final warning
that she wasn't to leave the house. Jane got busy with
housework that had been neglected since the week before.
Four loads of laundry and a clean refrigerator later, she
detected the faint burnt-dust odor that signified the furnace had kicked on for the first time in the season. She'd
always liked that smell. It meant sweaters and leaf-burning
and Christmas shopping and roast pork on Sundays.

Jim emerged from the basement with soot on his face
and grease on his fingers. Humming, Jane fixed him coffee
and warmed up a cinnamon roll snack while he went out
to his car to bring in a briefcase full of paperwork. As soon
as he was settled in the living room, she went to her
bedroom and made a duty call to Thelma. As she talked
with the phone clamped between her ear and shoulder,
she went through her lingerie drawer, culling the worst of
the dingy white-cotton atrocities.

The day dragged on. Jane got out to run across the
street with the recipe card she had promised to return to
Mary Ellen, but even that wasn't easy. "Take it back some
other time," Uncle Jim advised.

"I have a premonition that this is the last time I'll
ever see it. Things like this evaporate in my kitchen.
Besides, I won't be in any danger."

"What makes you think that?"

"You tell me how somebody with the use of only one

arm could strangle someone with a vacuum cleaner cord and I'll stay home."

"It's not what might happen to you there that worries me. It's the getting there!"

"Uncle Jim!"

"All right! Go!"

She sensed that he was watching her through the front window, so she made it a short visit. She was amused to have caught Mary Ellen, one of the neatest people she knew, with a newspaper and scraps of paper all over the coffee table. Probably cutting out coupons, Jane thought, and smiled a little. Who would have guessed a woman so glossy and professional would cut out grocery store coupons just like normal people?

"Jane, what's happening about that horrible murder?" she asked, scooping up the papers with her good hand as if embarrassed at being caught at such a mundane task.

"I don't know and I don't want to know," Jane said firmly. "It's none of my business. It's up to the police. I've got to get home," she said, suddenly depressed at how this thing had come to be the core of all her conversations. What did they all used to talk about?

Shelley came over and had lunch with them, and persuaded Jim to let Jane go to the grocery store with her. Jane came back and spent the afternoon cooking. Reluctantly, Jim agreed to let Jane pick up Todd's car pool, as long as she took Shelley along. Just as she was leaving, the red MG pulled up.

"I just got a call from your uncle to come talk to him. Why didn't you tell me Jim Spelling was your uncle?"

"You didn't ask and he isn't really. Why? Do you know him?"

"No, but I've heard of him. I'm really looking forward to hearing what he thinks of all this."

She let him in the house and went to get Shelley. "He's looking forward to hearing what Uncle Jim has to say," she told her friend. "I don't like it. That means he needs help."

Shelley was cranky. "I'm never going to get my children back. I hope my sister remembers to invite me to their graduations and weddings. I'd have them home now except for Paul. I'm concerned for their safety. He's fanatic about it."

She was quiet the rest of the way. Jane crammed her grade-schoolers into the back seat and got them all dropped off without Shelley saying another word. When they finally got home, Todd scrambled out and the two women stayed in the car. The MG was gone.

Jane broke the silence. "We have to do something, don't we?"

"I thought you were cured of snooping."

Jane lit her first cigarette of the afternoon and considered it. "I thought so too. But this isn't getting resolved. At least when we meddled something *happened*, even if it was awful."

"You promised your uncle you'd behave."

"I know I did. But now we know to be more careful."

"So, what'll we do?"

"I don't know. Let's think about it, and I'll come over later tonight."

"He'll let you out of the house?"

"I'll claim I have to borrow some personal, female thing that he'll be embarrassed to question. Of course, he'll probably stand at the door and watch me cross the driveways. Maybe hold my hand and walk me across."

For the second night, the children stayed home to enjoy the rare treat of having Uncle Jim around. About eight o'clock, Jane made her escape. As she predicted, he did stand at the door and watch until she was safely inside Shelley's house.

"Where's Paul?" she whispered as she came in.

"Not to worry. He had to go back down to the office. One of the franchisees got flooded out this afternoon and he's wrangling with the insurance people. So, what have you come up with?"

"You first."

"I asked first."

"Well—" Jane sat down, elbows on the table and chin in hands. "This might sound sort of absurd, but my thinking is, nothing's happening. Obviously everybody's got some kind of secret, right? We've found out what a few of them are already, and we could go on nosing around orever and all we'd find out is more secrets—*not* who's willing to kill somebody to keep them. Right?"

"Right. Go on." Shelley was sitting across from her in a mirror-image attitude. She'd been nodding the whole time Jane talked.

"So, if we go on, we might just make everybody mad without solving anything. And it's possible—probable— that we've already questioned the person responsible, and it would be a waste of time too. Shelley, I don't think this is a confirmed murderer, somebody with a mad bloodlust. It could be a once-in-a-lifetime thing. So, the way I see it, there's one logical way to find out who tried to kill Edith and accidentally killed the other woman."

Shelley nodded again. "To give her another shot at it . . ."

"Exactly. All we have to do is recreate the same circumstances. That's what you came up with too, wasn't it?"

"Yes. But there are two big problems. First, Edith isn't working this week. There's no way we'd get her to cooperate with this. Don't forget, she's as much a criminal in her own way as the killer. She's hardly going to willingly become bait for her own blackmail victim."

"Yes, but if you insist—Shelley, you can do it. You're the best 'insister' I know."

Shelley shook her head emphatically. "That gets us to the second problem. I have a strong premonition that the police aren't going to welcome this solution. It just doesn't seem the tried and true method."

"But, Shelley, I've got that figured out too. This is the sneaky part you're going to love. We don't tell them!"

Shelley sat back, shaking her head. "No way. We can't stage this whole thing by ourselves. For one thing, I just want the criminal caught: I don't want to do the catching myself."

"No, wait! I didn't mean we *never* tell the police. I just meant we set it all up and *then* tell them."

"Hmmm—not bad. So we get the story out that the house is going to be empty with only Edith here, then we suggest to the cops that they take it from there? They can't tell me I *can't* tell people anything I want, can they? And once it's already set up, they might use the opportunity, no matter how irregular they think it is."

"Sure. We've got nothing to lose."

"Jane, we have *everything* to lose. But I want the killer arrested so I can have my family back. All right. How do we get everybody here?"

"I've got some ideas on that . . ."

Within fifteen minutes they had a story worked out. "Who do we try it on first?"

"How about Mary Ellen Revere? She's not mad at us yet."

"Good enough. She's smart. If we can fool her, we can fool anybody."

Shelley picked up the phone, dialed, and said, "Mary Ellen? Shelley. With all the horrible stuff that happened last week, I lost sight of the fact that we're supposed to turn in a report on the committee's work on that playground project. I'm afraid we really do need to have a meeting as soon as possible— That's nice of you, but I can have it here—I'd like to try again for this Thursday night, that's the best night for me— Yes, potluck again, just bring the same thing I assigned last week. That's less confusing— Good. Now, there's one little difficulty, and I'm a little embarrassed to tell you. It's really a bit ghoulish—"

She looked over at Jane and crossed her fingers as she went on. "Jane and I promised to take her aunt in Evanston to the doctor that day, so neither of us will be around— No, it takes both of us. The poor old dear is in a wheelchair— Yes, in Evanston. You haven't ever heard Jane mention her? That's funny, it seems to me that she talks about her all the time—"

She listened for a minute, looked uncomfortable, and said, "I guess I don't either sometimes. Now, the house will be open, of course. It's Edith's day. What?— She's not? Well, she'd better come here on Thursday. I paid in advance for the first month, and the Happy Helper people are going to give me what I paid for or I'll know the reason why!"

Jane nervously paced around the kitchen while Shelley finished up the call. When Shelley hung up, she pounced. "It worked!"

"She was pissed that I was going to have Edith, come hell or high water, when she couldn't get her this week, but I think I convinced her I could do it."

"What was that other stuff? About me and my fictional aunt in Evanston?"

Shelley laughed. "She said she probably hadn't been paying attention when you mentioned her, and went on to say that she often tuned you out because you talk so much."

"And I thought she was hanging on my every word," Jane said, smiling. "All right. Who's next?"

"Why don't I go down the list and call you when I'm done? You better go home before he sends the National Guard to fetch you."

"Right. Shelley, this *is* going to work, isn't it?"

"It better, or we're going to both have to move to Alaska to escape our neighbors and the wrath of the police."

The phone rang at 10:10.

"I'll get it upstairs," Jane said, sprinting up the steps, leaving Uncle Jim and the kids looking at her like she'd gone around the bend.

"Sorry it took me so long. I couldn't get Suzie until a few minutes ago," Shelley began.

"So, did they all buy it?"

"All but Suzie. She just laughed and said, 'Ah-hah! A trap!' and when I said I had no idea what she meant, she said, 'I didn't come to town on a turnip truck, but I'll play along anyway.' But she wasn't the worst."

"Robbie?"

"You betcha. I think she believed it, but she didn't like it. She would have hung up, but I talked so fast she didn't have a chance. I apologized up a storm and said we'd just gone temporarily insane from the stress and we'd never do a thing like that again."

"Did she forgive us?"

"Not so's you'd notice."

"She agreed to come?"

"Only out of duty. She said she'd made a moral

commitment to the playground, otherwise she'd never se
foot in my home again. In the end, she paraphrase
Nixon. She said when the committee work was done, w
wouldn't have Robbie to kick around any more."

"What does that mean?"

"I have no idea, Jane, but it made me feel like shit.

"What about our friend Lucrezia Greenway?"

"Huh? Oh, Joyce. You're speaking figuratively agai
No wonder Mary Ellen doesn't listen to you half the time
Say—poison! What an awful idea. What if one of ther
brings poisoned food?"

"Now whose imagination is running away with them?
She heard someone coming up the stairs and lowered he
voice. "What about Joyce?"

"She agreed to come, and even to bring food, but
had to lie and say you couldn't attend the meeting. Doroth
Wallenberg must have been busy with something else
'cause she didn't even question the idea. She just said
'Yes, yes, all right. Let me write it on my calenda
Good-bye.'"

"Who's left? Oh, Laura Stapler. I'll bet she was craz
about it."

"Nearly wet her pants. I could tell over the phone. I
was a tough fight, and I nearly bought a security syster
before it was over. She eventually agreed to come, bu
said she'd probably have her husband bring her dish fo
her."

"So we've got it all set up. Now all we have to do i
tell the police."

There was a long silence on the other end.

"Shelley?"

"Yeah. Who's going to do that? I've already called th
committee. And I'm the one who has to arrange to ge
Edith here. I think it's your turn."

"Shelley, I'll never ask you to give me anothe
permanent."

"Not good enough."

"I'll drive all your car pools the week before Christ
mas when the kids are berserk."

"Getting closer."

"I'll give you all my grocery store coupons."

"They're probably outdated."

"Oh, all right." She took a deep breath and said, miserably, "I'll take your place as fifth-grade room-mother."

"All of the above."

"Yes."

"It's a deal. I'll call in and report what we've set up first thing in the morning. No point in ruining the whole night for our poor Detective VanDyne. I'll call you when I've talked to him."

"There won't be any need. The shock waves will probably flatten my house."

Chapter Twenty-two

She was right.

All went well enough through the morning rush. Shelley called to say she'd talked to the Happy Helper people and they'd promised to deliver Edith the next day. Jane started to ask her how she'd managed it, but refrained. Shelley's methods were sometimes better left unexamined. It was enough that she'd accomplished her goal. By the time everyone was off to school and the animals fed, Jane started getting nervous. Uncle Jim was going to work today, and was downing the last of his French toast when the phone rang. A vaguely familiar and frigidly cold voice asked for him, a voice that sounded suspiciously like Detective VanDyne in a very poor frame of mind.

Jane silently handed Jim the phone and suddenly remembered something urgent she had to do in the backyard. She wished she had some pressing errand in a foreign country, but the backyard would have to do.

She was pretending to weed under the fir tree when Uncle Jim came out. His tie was askew, his scowl as fierce as any she'd ever seen. His movements were deliberate. He picked up a patio chair and banged the front legs on the cement to dislodge some loose leaves. It looked like he was trying to destroy it. He sat down, leaned back, pointed a finger at her, and then jabbed it toward another chair.

"Sit!"

"Detective VanDyne is a tattletale," she said, perching on the edge of the chair he'd indicated.

"A grown woman," he said, shaking his head sadly. "The mother of three fine, fatherless children."

"If it weren't me involved, you'd think this was really quite a good idea. I'm sure if you'd just consider it dispassionately—"

The last word was hardly out of her mouth before he leaned forward so quickly she thought he was jumping at her throat. "Jane, this is the goddamnedest, stupidest, most dangerous idea I've ever heard from a pair of pea-brained females..."

He went on at some length and with a fluency that surprised her. When he'd finally run out of steam, Jane said quietly, "But the police are going to help us, aren't they?"

"Help you? The *police* help *you*?" He threw his hands up in the air in a gesture of furious despair, got up, and stomped inside the house.

"Aren't they?" she persisted, following him. "Uncle Jim, if this isn't resolved, I'll live the rest of my life afraid that somebody is going to change her mind about stabbing mattresses and stab me instead—or the kids. I see these women all the time, and I probably will for years to come. Suppose I say something in all innocence that the murderer assumes to mean that I know something? It simply has to be brought to a head. Come on, you agree with that, don't you?"

He glared at her, his face red. "Mel VanDyne is on his way over. You go to your friend Shelley's and both of you stay there and wait. Don't touch the phone. Don't touch a car key. Don't try to figure anything out. Don't think. Don't talk!"

"Yes, sir," she said and bounded out the door before he could change his mind.

Shelley was hovering in her kitchen, waiting. "I saw you out in back getting yelled-out."

"It's going to work, Shelley. I'm sure of it. If we insist on going through with it, they'll have to at least provide us with police protection, and if they're going to be here anyway, well..."

They waited nearly an hour, then Jim Spelling and Mel VanDyne came over, looking like angry pallbearers.

The first twenty minutes were wasted on trying to con
vince Jane and Shelley that their plan was insane. "You
don't even know this cleaning lady was the intended
target," VanDyne said.

"She had to have been. And if you didn't believe it,
why have you been asking all these questions about her
and the neighbors?" Jane asked.

"I've asked a lot of people a lot of questions," VanDyne
snapped. "This is one line of inquiry. I've got men out
pursuing several other lines as well, and I don't intend to
pull them off their work to help you conduct this little
farce of yours!"

"That's quite all right," Shelley said calmly. "We're
going to do it anyway, with or without you. We just
thought it was fair to tell you, in case you wanted to
participate in catching the murderer."

Finally the two men realized it was hopeless and went
on to the next stage.

"All right, Janey," Uncle Jim said, narrowing his eyes
menacingly. "Here are the ground rules. Mr. Nowack has
to agree to it first—"

"I'm sure he will," Shelley said, looking not at all
sure.

"Most important, you two women will be out of here
from the moment the cleaning lady arrives until it's all
over with. Out of the houses, out of the neighborhood, if
possible, out of the state! Do you understand that? And I
mean *truly* understand! No clever little tricks, no last-
minute changes in plan."

Jane and Shelley exchanged looks. "Sure," Jane said.

"All right," VanDyne said. "Here's the plan then.
We'll get some men in here tonight. As soon as Mr.
Nowack and all of Mrs. Jeffry's children are gone in the
morning, you two will make a big public production of
leaving. You'll stay away all day."

"But I have to pick my kids up from school," Jane
protested.

"You can pick them up, but arrange to take them
somewhere else. Didn't you mention a mother-in-law?
Give me her name and number. We'll call you both there

when it's all over. If—and it's a big if—anything happens at all, which I very seriously doubt."

He can claim he doubts all he wants, Jane thought, *but if he doesn't really believe it will work, why are they so vehement about us leaving?* "Sounds fine with me. Shelley?"

"Okay. Now will you call my husband or shall I?"

Having stirred up so much trouble, Jane felt it imperative to be a model of domesticity the rest of the day. She stayed home, ironing and cleaning, and even arranged a peaceful little tableau to greet Uncle Jim when he got home late that afternoon. An early fall fire burned in the fireplace; the dog snored at her feet as she sat mending a pair of his socks. She'd have to hide them and buy a new pair before he could see her handiwork. Having never darned socks in her life, she wasn't doing a very good job. The children hung around all evening, so the subject of Thursday's plans didn't come up.

Wednesday passed in the same way. Afraid she'd somehow give the game away if she talked to anybody, Jane kept to the house. Only one strange incident marked the day. Around lunchtime the phone rang, but when she answered, the caller hung up. A half an hour later it rang again, and after a long silence there was something like a sob and then a click and a dial tone. Jane tried to convince herself it was Joyce Greenway trying to make an approach and unable to pull herself together. But she was still troubled.

She dialed Joyce's number, just to see who would answer, but no one did.

About nine o'clock that evening, Willard's head suddenly came up from between his feet, and he howled horribly before running for cover. "What was that?" Uncle Jim asked.

"It sounded like a knock at the patio door!" Jane said, hearing nothing now but the pounding of her own heart in her ears.

Uncle Jim went to investigate and came back looking

disgusted. "Damned fools came to the wrong house. There's no hope in hell for this."

She assumed he meant the officers who were supposed to be sneaked into Shelley's house. "Why the back door?"

"Because they came across that field out back."

Mike, who'd been sprawled in front of the fire reading *Great Expectations*, was now watching them with open curiosity. It was time to explain to him. Leaving out the specifics of the blackmail and the whole episode of the paring knife in the mattress, Jane gave him a summary of the plan for tomorrow. "You can see that it's very important that none of you change plans and come home until we know it's safe. You *must* wait for me to pick you up from school."

He took it very well. She could never be sure when his maturity was going to come through and when it was going to crumble. "Sure, Mom. And Todd'll do what he's told without having to know why. But what about Katie? You never know where she'll turn up. I know! I'll tell her Johnny Hervey is coming home with us in the car; she'd wait forever so she wouldn't miss the chance to sit next to him in the backseat."

"Who in the world is Johnny Hervey?"

"You don't know him, but she does," he said with a leer.

Jane went to bed early, but slept fitfully. She kept hearing the middle-of-the-night creaks the house made and imagining sinister happenings. What would happen tomorrow? Had she and Shelley really made the horrible mistake Uncle Jim and Mel VanDyne claimed? What if it didn't work? Would they ever know which of their friends was a killer, or would they just go from day to day and year to year wondering . . . always wondering?

Chapter Twenty-three

She was awake long before the alarm went off. Going downstairs, she peeked out the windows at the Nowack's house and the street. Everything looked absolutely normal. As soon as it was fully light, Paul came out, backed the car to the end of the driveway, then got out and returned to the house for his briefcase. Jane wondered if that was for real or planned to make sure any possible watcher was thoroughly aware of his leaving.

Jane drove Katie to cheerleading practice, came back and took the boys to band practice, and was home before Todd was picked up. "Hey, Mom, old thing. You look kinda sick or something," he said as Dorothy Wallenberg's Mazda pulled up.

"Just tired, Todd, old thing. I'll take a nap today and be gorgeous by this afternoon."

Dorothy just waved to her and drove off when Todd got in the car. Apparently this wasn't going to be an exact replica of the last time or she'd have had her cake along.

Back inside, Uncle Jim was opening a can of cat food, having taken seriously his role as member of the family. "What'll you do?" she asked him.

"As soon as you two leave, I'll slip across to Nowack's behind that hedge."

"So you think it's a near neighbor—Laura or Suzie or somebody on the block who can see the house, instead of Robbie?"

"It's possible."

She had a feeling he knew more than he was telling

her, but this wasn't the time to try to pry anything out of him—not that she'd have any success anyway.

A few minutes later a blue Happy Helper van stopped in front of Shelley's. There was only one person besides the driver. The door opened and Edith got out. Jane had been afraid she wouldn't show up, in spite of Shelley's efforts.

At nine-thirty, Jane strolled across the two driveways and knocked on Shelley's door. "Come in," Shelley said.

"Where's Edith?" Jane asked.

"Upstairs in the master bedroom with an officer, being questioned and kept out of sight."

There was the sound of heavy footsteps in the room above, a male voice mumbling from the basement stairway, and Mel VanDyne and another man were in the living room, talking quietly over some paper work. He looked up at the sound of Jane's voice. "Ah, Mrs. Jeffry. Are you ready to leave?" He sounded cranky.

"No, I'm not leaving," Jane said.

"What?" Shelley and VanDyne spoke in unison.

"This is my idea and I'm going to see it through," Jane insisted.

"Oh, it's your idea, all right," VanDyne drawled sarcastically, "but you're not seeing it through. In fact, if you don't get out of here right now, I'll have you arrested and taken away for interfering with an officer doing his duty."

"Jane, be sensible," Shelley implored. "If we aren't seen leaving, it'll wreck the plan. The whole point is to make it appear Edith is here alone. Come along right now!"

Jane might have marshaled a further argument, except at that moment her attention was diverted to a figure at the head of the stairway. Edith. No, not Edith. A woman with blond frizzy hair and a Happy Helper uniform that looked very much like the cleaning lady. "Hey, Mel, what time you got?" the figure said in a deep, male voice.

"That's a man!" Jane exclaimed.

"You didn't think they'd let the murderer actually attack Edith, did you?" Shelley asked. In a single, quick motion, she grabbed Jane's arm and steered her out the kitchen door before she could protest.

As per their instructions, they dawdled along, taking their time getting into Jane's station wagon. Shelley stopped and pointed to Jane's house and pretended to talk about the roof. Then they turned and looked at Shelley's roof. All this was to make sure that anyone who might be watching didn't miss their departure.

While they stood there, Mary Ellen Revere emerged from her house to get the paper and waved with her good arm. Suzie Williams tooted the horn merrily as she passed on her way to work. The Staplers' house showed no signs of life. Nor could Jane recognize any of the cars parked here and there along the street as suspicious.

At a discreet hand sign from Jane's kitchen window, she and Shelley got in the car and drove off. "Where are we going?" Shelley asked.

Jane didn't answer for a minute, then said, "Anywhere we want, just so they think we've gone, but we're coming back. I want to see what happens and make sure VanDyne doesn't screw anything up."

"If he heard you say that, he'd probably shoot you. I'm not sure I'd blame him. We are *not* going back until it's over."

"But Shelley—"

"No 'buts.' Consider yourself taken captive. I won't take you back there."

They stopped at a fast-food drive-through and got danishes and coffee. Jane reluctantly dragged out a city map and pretended to look it over for possible destinations. "I know," Shelley said. "I know where there's a gardening supply store. Let's go look at bulbs and seeds and things. By the time we get there, have a nice look around and long lunch someplace, and then drive home, that ought to effectively eat up most of the day. Take a left out of here and then a right at the next stop light."

Jane opened her mouth to make one last appeal to return to the stakeout, but Shelley's warning glance froze the words in her throat. When Shelley got that look, there was no changing her mind.

In spite of her worries about what was going on back at

home, Jane managed to get into the spirit of shopping. A clerk was eager to help her, and unwilling to let her buy more than she could handle in the first year of gardening. Jane started accumulating little bags of bulbs that soon grew to an armful. When she dropped one, the clerk said, "Let's find something to put those in."

Near them on the floor there was a big, round-bottomed stainless steel mixing bowl someone had used to clean up some spilled potting soil. Flecks still adhered to the inside. "Bulbs won't mind a little dirt. The outside is clean," the clerk said, holding it while Jane dumped her purchases in.

As he handed it to her, she realized too late that the outside of the bowl was a little damp and very slippery. It was also heavier than she anticipated, and slithered out of her grip. The bowl bounced, clanging, on the cement floor, and bulbs flew every which way.

"Oh, I'm so sorry, ma'am. I thought you had a hold of it," the clerk said, immediately stooping and starting to gather up the bulbs.

Jane and Shelley joined him on the floor. "It's not your fault," Shelley soothed. "She did the same thing in my kitchen the other day, but it was potato salad. A lot messier."

Something started whirring and clicking in the back of Jane's mind.

"Jane, you could at least help," Shelley said.

"I dropped the potato salad bowl!" Jane said, sitting back on her heels and putting her hands over her eyes to shut out everything so she could listen to what was going on in her brain.

"Well, it's no big deal. It didn't break. Jane, are you crying or something?"

"No, I'm thinking."

The clerk, by now, was looking uneasy. He put the last of the bulbs in the bowl and backed up as if ready to make a run for safety.

"Do you have a phone book here?" Jane asked him suddenly.

"Uh—yes, I think so. I'll get it for you."

"Jane, what is it?" Shelley asked.

"I'm not sure. Just let me think this out."

The clerk came back with the phone book, eyeing her nervously. Ignoring him, Jane starting flipping through pages. She found what she wanted and ran her finger down the column. Shelley looked over her shoulder. "Hospitals? What do you want to find a hospital for?"

"It's not here, Shelley. *It's not here!*"

The clerk was looking around frantically, ready to summon help if she got violent. Shelley grabbed her shoulder and shook her. "Jane, what in hell are you carrying on about?"

Jane rummaged in her purse and pulled out a five-dollar bill, which she handed to the astonished clerk. "I'm sorry, but I can't take time to buy these things today. I'll be back next week. This is for all your time and trouble. Come on, Shelley, I'll explain in the car."

As soon as the doors closed, Jane started rattling off her thoughts so fast Shelley could hardly understand her. When she'd wound down enough for Shelley to get a word in, she said, "I don't know, Jane—"

"But it has to be. Don't you remember the order those dishes were stacked in the refrigerator? This is the only thing that could possibly explain it! We've been wrong all along about Robbie. We have to tell VanDyne before it's too late. Suppose they think it was Robbie too, and come jumping out from behind the drapes and arrest her? It would be horrible for her, and it would blow the whole plan besides."

"How do you intend to contact him? The only person who's supposed to be at my house is Edith, and I don't think the police will risk answering the phone."

"Shelley—"

"*No, Jane.* We promised we wouldn't go back. We promised!"

"Haven't we already done enough to Robbie? Could you ever face yourself again if she got arrested by mistake and we could have stopped it? After all she's already been through? Shelley, I'm going back. You can come with me or not."

"Dammit, Jane! All right. But we can't just drive up. We'd spoil the stakeup."

"It's stake*out*. No, we'll get there the same way those men did last night. Across the field behind our houses."

"They did it at night when they couldn't be seen."

"*We* won't be seen either. It's tall grass. We'll crawl." She turned on the ignition and started home.

"You're insane!" Shelley shrieked, but Jane paid no attention.

It seemed a much longer trip back. Jane's driving, already frantic, wasn't improved when she realized she'd taken a wrong exit and made a U-turn on the highway to correct her error. When they finally stopped on the shoulder of the road, Shelley was shaking.

"If you think I'm going to ruin this outfit by crawling clear across—"

"No need, Shelley. It just takes one of us to explain," Jane said. She leaped out of the car and dived into the high grass before Shelley could change her mind. She'd never realized how large this field really was until she crossed it on her hands and knees. Nor did she have any idea previously of how many nasty, prickly things grew in it. Her arms and face were crosshatched with scratches by the time she reached the edge of Shelley's backyard.

She climbed over the fence and ran for the house, then flung herself down the basement stairwell and paused to get her breath for a moment before trying the door. Thank God! It was unlocked. She stepped in, picking her way carefully through Shelley's basement and up the stairs. At the top, she waited, listening. She didn't want to suddenly appear in Shelley's kitchen right in the midst of an arrest. Nor did she want to spring the trap too soon.

Finally, hearing nothing whatsoever, she gingerly pushed the door open a crack. Nothing. Open a little bit more. Still nothing. She stuck her head through and a voice next to her ear said, "Stop right there!"

She turned and looked into the barrel of a gun. Behind it there was a young man in jeans and a T-shirt that said "Tit for Tat."

Dear God! Had she been even more wrong than she thought? Had it been a wandering maniac after all? And why was he back here today? Would Thelma get to raise her children now?

"We got her, sir!" he shouted.

Suddenly the room was full of men. Five other plainclothesmen—including Detective Mel VanDyne and Uncle Jim Spelling, who emerged from the broom closet spitting flame. "Jesus Christ, Janey!" Uncle Jim said. "Put that gun down, Harris. She's not the one. Not that she doesn't deserve to be shot!"

Detective VanDyne had bent over the counter and looked like he was about to start banging his head on the Formica. "I could have gone into the family's hardware business, but no-o-o, I had to go into law enforcement . . ."

Harris, the wandering, maniac, put away his gun and turned. The back of his shirt said, "Okay, what's a Tat?"

"Uncle Jim, we were wrong. It isn't Robbie at all—"

At that moment, everyone froze at the sound of the vacuum cleaner starting upstairs. It was obviously a signal. The men in the kitchen instantly melted away. "I don't have room for her with me," Uncle Jim said. "You take her!" With that, he got in the broom closet and closed the door behind himself.

Mel VanDyne grabbed Jane's wrist and dragged her into the living room. Two sofas faced each other in front of the fireplace. VanDyne crouched behind the farthest one and yanked Jane down beside him. "Not a word! Don't even breathe!" he said.

"But you have to know someth—"

"Shut up!"

Jane caught her breath. Someone had opened the kitchen door. She started to peek over the top of the sofa, but VanDyne grabbed her hair with one hand and put the other over her mouth. She subsided.

The sound of high heels on the kitchen floor. The refrigerator door opening. The rattle of a dish lid. The refrigerator door closing.

Jane was sitting cross-legged on the floor, facing the back of the sofa and wishing she could see. Was her theory right? It had to be. It was the right dishwasher and the wrong dishes.

There was a long silence. The outside door should have opened by now if it was just somebody innocently delivering food and then leaving. The footsteps started

again, across the kitchen floor toward the living room.
When they hit carpet, they turned into soft scuffs. Jane
froze.

This was it. This was the murderer! Suddenly Jane
was very, very sorry she'd come back. There was almost
nowhere in the world she wouldn't rather be. Jane couldn't
hear the footsteps anymore. Was she walking to the stairway now, going up to try again to kill Edith? Beside her,
she felt Detective VanDyne stiffen, bunching his muscles
as if to spring.

She closed her eyes for a moment. Suddenly the sofa
moved a little, as if the killer had decided to sit down for a
minute and think about what to do next. Horrified, Jane
glanced at VanDyne. He was looking up. She followed his
gaze and found herself looking into a familiar face.

"What the fuck are you two doing back there?" Suzie
Williams asked.

Chapter Twenty-four

"You have the right to remain silent—"

"No! Stop!" Jane exclaimed.

"—If you give up that right—"

"She's not the one! Stop saying all that stuff!" Jane grabbed VanDyne's arm.

He pulled away. "Mrs. Jeffry, you are interfering—"

"Please listen. She's not the murderer. I swear it. But if we stand around making all this noise, we might scare off the person who is."

Again the men filled the room. The vacuum cleaner stopped.

"Have I interrupted something?" Suzie asked, throwing a dazzling smile at the one who'd put the gun in Jane's face. He puffed up his chest and smiled back.

"Mrs. Jeffry, I think you've gone crazy!" VanDyne snapped, his professional manner crumbling. "If you don't get out of here right this minute—"

"May I come in?" Shelley said from the basement door. Her clothes were a mess, and there were little green stick-tights spangling her hair.

"Oh, shit!" VanDyne said.

A voice from the top of the stairs said urgently, "Here comes another one, Mel."

"Look, there isn't time to explain, but it all makes complete sense," Jane said quickly. "Just trust me."

"Trust you? *You?*"

"Please. Just until whoever this is has come and gone. I'll tell you the whole thing and you'll see I'm right. I promise. If you don't agree, I'll sneak back out and not say another word."

VanDyne stared at her for a long moment, then at Suzie, who was smiling seductively. He looked like he half believed Jane and half wanted to shake her teeth loose.

Everyone stood, petrified, waiting for his decision. Finally he said, through gritted teeth, "It's only a career. What the hell!"

Swiftly, the man in the "Tit for Tat" shirt abandoned his study of Suzie and all but tackled Shelley, shoving her ahead of himself back down the basement stairs. Jane grabbed Suzie's hand and ran around behind the sofa. Mel VanDyne was just behind them. They crouched down, VanDyne between them. With the addition of Suzie's gorgeous but substantial presence, it was a very tight squeeze, and in spite of the emotion of the moment, Jane couldn't help but notice how very nice he smelled.

"If it's Robbie, you can't arrest her!" Jane whispered to him.

"*Shhh—*"

"But you've got to listen. There's no hospital in Oakview, don't you see? And the plastic wrap on the top of Suzie's bowl wasn't even dented."

"Be quiet!"

The house fell silent as the kitchen door opened. Again, there was the soft click of footsteps, then the refrigerator door opened. Jane could hear the sound of a dish being removed from the middle shelf and being set on the counter while the larger bowl was put in place. Yes, yes. She'd been right. That's how it had happened before— impossibly happened. A *klunk*. The heavy bowl, then Suzie's put back in. Jane was thinking of what the teacher had told the blind kids: See with your ears!

Jane held her breath. Mel VanDyne, crouched between them with a protective arm over each—*was* it protective, or was he just keeping them in place?—was so tense, she could almost feel the electricity of his nerves.

The refrigerator door closed and the footsteps, surprisingly firm—no hesitating, no reconsidering—went across the living room and up the stairs. Mel VanDyne was smiling as he rose, silent and lithe as a cat. He put a finger to his lips and gestured to them to stay put. Suzie and Jane peered over the top of the sofa as he moved across the room. "That's a *man*!" Suzie whispered.

Suddenly there was the sound of struggle upstairs. Shouts. A woman's scream. Uncle Jim leaped from the closet and headed for the stairs. The "Tit for Tat" man sprang from the basement door and followed. There was a terrible thump, as if someone had thrown the vacuum cleaner, still humming, at a wall.

"God!" Suzie whispered. Her normal high coloring had turned to the yellow-white of parchment. Jane felt sick. Not since the week before had she been truly conscious of the shock of real violence. Most of the time since then, this had been a mental problem. A puzzle of sorts. Very serious, very personal and emotional—God, yes. But not physical.

Jane saw Shelley emerge from the basement and start toward them. She shouldn't do that. Not until it was over. Jane rose to gesture her back, but Shelley was looking toward the stairway and the sounds of her house being torn up. Jane didn't want to shout at her. Even with all the noise upstairs, she might be heard. If she messed this up now, her uncle and Mel VanDyne would never get over it. She waved her arms, hoping to get Shelley's attention, but Shelley had stopped in the middle of the room, her eyes and ears locked in horror on the stairway. Jane crept around the end of the sofa and headed for her.

She'd almost reached Shelley when there was a pounding on the stairs, more shouting, bodies hurtling down. Jane whirled just as Mary Ellen Revere, on a dead run with Mel VanDyne only inches behind her, raised her arm in its cast and swung it at Jane's head.

Jane ducked, and Mary Ellen, her fierce swing unstopped, spun around and into VanDyne's arms. She struggled with insane strength for a moment, then suddenly seemed to crumple with exhaustion. Within seconds three men, including Uncle Jim, had hold of her, and VanDyne was barking into a walkie-talkie he'd taken out of his jacket pocket.

Behind them, a man in a Happy Helper uniform was coming down the stairs. His wig had gone askew and the stuffing in his shirt had shifted and he had one "breast" down at his waist. He was rubbing his throat. The "Tit for Tat" man was gallantly helping Suzie up from her position behind the sofa. Jane could hear sirens in the distance.

Mary Ellen's face, as she raised her head and looked at Jane, was flushed. There were stark, white marks around her lips and nose. "You bitch! You knew all along, didn't you? I should have realized you couldn't be as dumb as you always act."

Jane felt seared by the venom in her voice. She turned away, shaking.

Edith was being led down the steps by a uniformed officer. She shook off his arm and shambled over to Mary Ellen. There was both hate and arrogance in her voice. "You think *she's* stupid! I never had it so easy as with you. If you ever get out of the clink again, you better not keep a scrapbook about your escape."

"Scrapbook?" Jane said. "Scrapbook! Of course. I thought she was cutting coupons, but she was adding newspaper articles about the murder to it."

A siren whooped to a stop in front of the house.

"*Did* you know all along?" Suzie asked her twenty minutes later when Mary Ellen and Edith had been taken away. Uncle Jim had gone along to get her booked. Mel VanDyne had stayed back with two officers who were filling out forms and putting things into little plastic bags. VanDyne had spent most of the intervening time on the phone, talking in an incomprehensible verbal shorthand. The man in the Happy Helper uniform was waiting for someone to bring his own clothes to him. Shelley had made him an ice pack for his throat.

"No, of course I didn't know all along," Jane replied. "But I see why Mary Ellen thought so. That morning, before it all happened, I went over there and said something about how I'd never had any bones broken, but I once pretended I did and made myself a plaster cast."

"Which is exactly what she'd done," Shelley added.

"So that's what tipped you off?" Suzie asked.

"Oh, no, that didn't occur to me until I was driving

back here. What made me realize it had to be her was dropping a bowl. Two bowls, actually. When Shelley and I cleaned out the refrigerator, I lost my grip on that big ceramic bowl of hers and dumped potato salad all over the kitchen. We should have both realized that if it was that hard to keep hold of the thing with two good hands, it would be absolutely impossible to keep a grip on it with one. It was heavy and slippery."

"And then there was the way it was in the refrigerator," Shelley said. "She put it in at the bottom of the stack of dishes because it was the biggest and heaviest—and probably to make it seem like it had gotten there first, even though she said she'd come right after you, Suzie. That meant she had to take the other things that had come first out, slide hers clear in, and put the others back. She couldn't have done it with her arm the way she claimed it was."

"I still don't really get it," Suzie said. "I had a broken arm once and I got used to doing all sorts of things with it. I used the cast almost like a tool. Pushing things around with it. Balancing things on it—"

Jane took the last crumpled cigarette out of the pack in her purse, and was irritated to notice that she was still shaking so badly she could hardly light it. "But that's when you got used to it. She was claiming to have only broken it the day before. And when I was over there that morning, she was doing a convincing job of acting like it was so excruciatingly painful that she couldn't so much as lift a recipe card with that hand. Besides, she went too far in making the story convincing, and told me how a man at the grocery store had been so nice and drove her to the Oakview Community Hospital to have her arm set. There isn't a hospital in Oakview."

"Also, the bowl had a plate for a lid," Shelley said. "It didn't even fit tightly, and the bowl had to be kept perfectly level or it slid off."

"What was that you were trying to tell the divine detective about my bowl?" Suzie asked.

"Again, she got carried away with her alibi. She said you had just left when she came over, but your bowl was on top of hers. She probably didn't know which thing you brought. But if she'd moved yours with one hand, she'd have had to stick her thumb through the plastic wrap."

Suzie made a few experimental motions with her hands, trying to get the feel of what Jane was saying, then nodded her comprehension.

"And then there was the dishwasher," Jane said.

"What dishwasher?" Suzie asked.

"The killer had apparently turned on the dishwasher to make it appear the cleaning lady had been killed only moments before Shelley got home. An alibi of sorts, to make it look like the people who brought their food early were in the clear. Of course, with her dish at the bottom of the stack, Mary Ellen looked like she'd come very early, and she said she did."

"But that could have been anyone."

"No, only someone who knew how to work the timer gadget. You don't have one of those, I don't, and Shelley doesn't even know how to work hers. But when I went to Mary Ellen's that morning, I noticed that she had the same kind. Well, I don't mean I noticed then, but I remembered later noticing what a complicated-looking control panel it had."

"She took an awful chance—" Suzie said.

"There must have been an awful need. Imagine planning something like that. She must have started thinking about it when Shelley told all of us she was going to be gone, but Edith would be here."

"But if anyone had seen her carrying the potato salad in both hands, it would have wrecked an alibi she'd gone to a lot of trouble to set up," Suzie said.

"And the chances were good that somebody would. She took a big risk. You know how snoopy everybody in this neighborhood is," Jane said.

"Do I ever!" Suzie said. "There are women around here who come right into your house and ask if you're being blackmailed."

Shelley got up and went to the kitchen. "The coffee's ready. Who wants some? Jane, I could give it to you in a big cup and maybe you could drown yourself."

"I'd like some, thanks, ma'am," the man in the Happy Helper uniform said. He'd managed to straighten out his bosom.

"I still don't see how she knew about your snooping," Shelley said.

"My snooping? You were in on it, as I recall," Jane said. She explained to Suzie, who was unaccountably blushing. "She stabbed a note, warning me to mind my own business, in my bed. Why are you that color, Suzie?"

"I guess I better confess. I told her. She called just after you left my house and I was still laughing my ass off about your clumsy attempts at detection. I guess we're even. You went looking for gossip and I kept busy spreading it. So, how did you and Shelley eliminate each other as suspects?"

"We never suspected each other for a minute," Jane declared.

"Come off it!"

"Never!" Jane insisted.

Shelley was smiling. "How *did* you know it wasn't me, Jane? I could have been lying about the airport and sneaked back across the field, like we did a while ago. You must have at least wondered, didn't you?"

Jane was afraid she might be blushing too. Shelley was expressing a thought that *had* crossed her mind. "Well, only occasionally. But in the end, I knew you wouldn't risk messing your house up. If you were going to kill somebody, you'd do it where you wouldn't have to clean up afterwards."

Shelley laughed. "And I knew it wasn't you because you couldn't sneak up on somebody without talking."

"So how did you find out what she was being blackmailed about?" Suzie asked.

"I didn't," Jane answered. She was smiling now too, relieved in a funny way that Shelley had briefly suspected her. It made her feel less guilty about thinking she or Suzie might have been a killer. "I didn't even think of trying to find out if Mary Ellen was being blackmailed. The broken-arm business had me so fooled I didn't even consider her. Besides, I'd already found out more than I wanted to about—about some other things. Isn't it strange? I thought we had to know what the blackmail was about,

when all we needed to know was right in Shelley's refrigerator. Still, I wonder. . ."

"Edith was telling the truth about a jailbreak," a voice
behind Jane said. VanDyne had come into the room on
that silent tread. He came around and sat down next to
Jane. She'd have been flattered except that it was the only
seat available. "We've run her through the computer.
She'd been a bank teller in California, and spent two years
in jail for embezzling. She was sentenced to three, but let
herself out early. Your cleaning lady was the only thing
between her and going back to jail."

"So what was the catalyst?" Jane asked.

"I thought you were the one with all the answers," he
said. His tone was light, with only the tiniest glimmer of
sarcasm coming through.

Jane gave him a level look for a long moment, then
said, "I don't know for sure. Maybe it was simply the first
opportunity she had that would leave her in the clear. She
couldn't very well kill the woman in her own house and
not have her past looked into. But killing her here, on a
day when half the neighborhood was due to pass through,
was perfect. I just wish I'd caught on sooner about the
scrapbook."

"A stupid thing to do, but human just the same,"
VanDyne mused. "It was her fifteen minutes of fame."

"Still, I wish I'd realized it then. I wouldn't have been
forced to crawl through that field and risk my life—!"

"If I recall correctly, I told you that you were not to
come back here under any circumstances," VanDyne said.

"Yes, but if I hadn't, you'd have arrested the wrong
person and wouldn't have caught Mary Ellen at all."

"If it weren't for your butting in, we wouldn't have
been conducting this comedy of errors at all. And sure,
we'd have gotten her. It was just a matter of time before
the computer would have spit out the information about
her in the normal course of the investigation—"

"But you wouldn't have caught her in the act of trying
it again! That was all our idea—"

"I'll say! And if you ask me—"

"I've got to get back to work," Suzie said, cutting the
squabble short. "You'll confirm to my boss why I took so

long, won't you?" she asked VanDyne, batting her eyes so
effectively that VanDyne dropped his dispute with Jane
and gave her his full attention.

Suzie had been gone only a minute when there was a
knock on the door, and Shelley let in a man in a police
uniform. He had a bundle of clothing for Edith's double
and a big, aromatic paper bag with a grease stain on the
bottom. "Here's your lunch," he said to Mel VanDyne.

"That's Chinese carryout!" Jane said.

"Right you are. My reward," VanDyne said, starting to
take little cartons out of the bag. "You want some?"

Jane was famished, but Suzie's mention of the time
had reminded her of her own responsibilities. "Thanks,
but I've got to go pick the kids up from school."

Shelley went to the door with her. "You'll come right
back, won't you?"

Jane looked over Shelley's shoulder into the living
room. Mel VanDyne smiled his dimpled smile and waved
at her with a pair of chopsticks.

"I might be a little while. I think I'll stop and buy a
wok and Chinese cookbook. Time I expanded a few of my
horizons, don't you think?"

ABOUT THE AUTHOR

JILL CHURCHILL is a pseudonym of historical novelist Janice Young Brooks. A mystery buff since her Nancy Drew days, one of her most treasured possessions is a personal letter from John Dickson Carr. She's currently between cleaning ladies.